Unbewitched

Devilish #7

Charity Parkerson

Punk & Sissy Publications

Copyright

Punk
&
Sissy

—Warning: This book is intended for readers over the age of 18. Some of my books contain allusions to past abuse and trauma.

Editor: BZ Hercules & Consultants

Cover art: Charity Parkerson

Contents

Introduction

A SUPERNATURAL PLAYER HAS met his match. Stone doesn't have time for this. Fate doesn't care.

Stone is well known for bed-hopping. No one expects more of him. That's a good thing, since he currently has a huge issue he needs to solve. Now is definitely not the time for his latest conquest to be his true mate. Especially since that mate is a needy fairy, and Stone is currently possessed by a dark entity he can't see to fight.

Copulation is very close to food for fairies. While they can't survive on that alone, they also don't thrive without it. Everyone knows they shouldn't take going to bed with a fairy seriously. Fairies certainly don't. That's why it took Lysander so long to figure out why he couldn't stay away from Stone. Of all the times to find his mate, this was the most unfortunate.

Unbewitched is the seventh book in Charity Parkerson's Devilish series, where vampires, Weres, demons, gods, and all manner of the supernatural live together beneath the noses of humankind. These books are best when read in order.

Chapter One

BRIGHT SUNLIGHT BURNED THROUGH the trees. The illusion of glitter hung in the air. The scent of fresh grass and flowers was all around. Lysander had always loved Faerie. This plane was the only real home he had ever known or cared to know. Plenty of his brethren had left over the years to make their way in the human world. Not Lysander. He enjoyed the occasional visit, and he understood what lured his kin. The way humans put their whole heart and soul into sex was irresistible to most fairies. It never took long for his kind to get addicted to that much energy being poured into them. While sex wasn't exactly their food, they still needed it to thrive and survive. He had heard tales of how love heightened the experience, making fairies glow like the sun. Lysander would never know.

He rolled onto his side in his magical hammock and skimmed his fingers through the creek below. Lysander wasn't being dramatic. He didn't feel all "woe is me" or anything like that. Lysander literally stood no chance of finding love. He already had an unclaimed mate. Fate had a cruel streak, it seemed. Lysander could never have his other half. The sound of trickling water didn't soothe him the way it usually did. Nothing did.

Lysander closed his eyes and pictured Stone—the sexy vampire life had chosen for him. His twinkling blue eyes and strawberry blond hair were such a gorgeous combination. Lysander's chest hurt. It had only been a week since Lysander had followed Stone through the woods. The memory would forever be seared into his mind.

No grass rustled. No twigs popped. Lysander's steps caused zero noise. Lysander was in the earthly realm, but then again, he wasn't. Faerie existed all around him. The two planes were one, but they weren't. Only certain creatures and those who ate food prepared by a fairy could see the seamless union. Stone had given up on food centuries ago, and Lysander hadn't allowed Stone to drink from him. Lysander easily stalked him through the woods without being seen.

While Lysander had no idea where Stone headed, he kept pace. He needed to know what Stone had done to him. Lysander was like any other fairy. His life revolved around sex. Just as a vampire needed blood to survive, Lysander required the lust-filled energy to thrive. Sex was rarely personal with his species. Unless they found their true mate, fairies were unabashed flirts and sexual creatures. Since Lysander had allowed Stone to seduce him, something changed inside him. His thoughts were mired in jealous rage. Stone was very similar to fairy folk. He didn't hide his base needs behind a veneer of fake relationship goals. He fucked like sex was his fuel, and Lysander hadn't been right since. Lysander didn't feel this driving need to own someone the way he did with Stone. He was furious and determined. Stone would lift this spell, or Lysander would see him dead to escape this hell.

Stone stepped around a large tree and disappeared.

Lysander froze and searched his senses. It was daytime. Vampires couldn't vanish in the daylight. It was further proof of Lysander's theory. Stone wasn't—

In a breathtaking jerk, Lysander was snatched from behind and found the bark of a tree digging into his back. With an outraged vampire boxing him against the tree, he could get away a dozen ways, but his body wouldn't obey.

"Why are you following me?" His fangs peeked out with each word, and Lysander was burning alive.

He licked his lips in his nervousness. His gaze wouldn't move from those damn fangs.

The need to feed had him in a chokehold. "You think too much of yourself. We're simply headed in the same direction."

A deadly-sounding chuckle left Stone's lips and tickled the base of Lysander's spine. "Is that so? Tell me, what place has you going my way?"

Dear King, Lysander's body begged to be touched. His throat no longer worked. He couldn't answer. Pure lust stole everything from him. As he stared into Stone's eyes, he realized the truth. Stone truly had ruined him for all others, and now he knew why. He stared into the face of his mate. Thankfully, or unfortunately, depending on how one looked at things, Stone didn't seem to realize the truth yet. That didn't stop Stone from leaning his weight into Lysander. His lips skimmed Lysander's. It was over as quickly as the kiss had started.

Stone shoved away from him and pushed Lysander in the opposite direction. "Get the fuck out of here. I don't want to look at your face anymore."

The words stung more than Lysander ever imagined. He had always thought his mate would at the very least find him attractive. While licking his wounds, Lysander used his magic to completely vanish.

Lysander still had a hot coal in his gut each time he thought about things. Not that it mattered how Stone felt about Lysander. They could never be true, fully claimed mates. He had been right about more than his inability to steer clear of Stone. That would be true of any mates. Unfortunately, he had also been right about vampires being unable to disappear in the daytime. Vampires couldn't do that. But a dark Fae could, and that was exactly what possessed Stone. Lysander had seen the beast in Stone's eyes. That wasn't something Stone could ever be freed from. He was as lost to Lysander as he would be if he had died. In fact, that was an apt description. Stone was dead. His body just didn't know it yet.

The room spun. A heavy copper taste coated the inside of his mouth. He couldn't recall what he had done last night. His guess was there was a lot of blood and sex involved. Stone's entire body stank. He stumbled his way to the bathroom. A quick glance in the mirror confirmed his thoughts. Dried blood coated his chin, and the distinct scent of pussy lingered on his fingers. Goddess, he was sick of himself. He had no clue why he couldn't recall a thing.

Stone stood under a deluge of hot water and zoned out. It took him a moment to come back to himself and scrub his body clean. It was a damn good thing vampires couldn't catch or spread diseases. This shit was out of control. An image of Lysander rose in his mind. Stone had him backed against a tree. Their lips met. A shaky-sounding breath was the only sound he could make. His entire body cramped with need. Stone had shoved away from him and told him he never wanted to see Lysander's face again. Why had he done that? Why did he barely remember seeing him at all? He already felt the memory slipping away from him. It was time to find Frost.

The town's healer Stone had been sent to protect had disappeared a while back.

It was Stone's job to protect him. He had no idea why he hadn't searched for Frost. When he thought about the past few months, there were only scattered memories littered throughout nothingness. That shit drove him insane, and scared the hell out of him, if he were being honest. Stone never disrespected his post. He was proud to be among Celeste's most trusted warriors. Something had to be seriously wrong with him. He had no excuse for not protecting Frost or searching the planet from top to bottom, leaving no stone unturned. Damn. Maybe he was dying. It was a damn good thing Frost had turned back up all on his own, like he had merely been on vacation. It didn't look as if he could depend on Stone.

Lysander's expression danced across Stone's brain. He had looked so hurt when Stone pushed him away. Stone rubbed his chest. Why had he done that? That was all he could think. The question haunted him. While Stone was definitely a fighter, he was very much a lover too. He didn't hurt his conquests. Not only that, but he also genuinely liked Lysander. They were supposed to be friends. It seemed as if Stone had failed everyone around him lately. He didn't even know where to start to fix things.

An image of Lysander floating above a beautiful creek flashed through Stone's mind. The scene felt so real. He closed his eyes and pressed his forehead against the shower wall. Stone focused everything he possessed on reclaiming the moment. Blinding, glittery light fell around him. He saw Lysander as clearly as he would if Lysander were actually there. Lysander was in full fairy form. His flawless body glimmered. Lysander's translucent wings drooped. Sadness washed over him. As he looked on, a tear fell from Lysander's eye and landed in the water. Lysander swatted the water as if trying to wipe away his reflection. Stone could barely breathe through the heavy emotions. Suddenly, Lysander rolled and their gazes met. The truth hit like a punch to his gut.

"Now, now. We don't wallow." The scene bled to black, suffocating him for a reason he couldn't see. Stone couldn't control his body. Everything became a blur. He didn't know who he was any longer, but he wasn't himself anymore.

Chapter Two

LYSANDER STARED AT THE empty space just feet from him. He hadn't imagined things. Stone had been there—half in Faerie and half out. It had been him, though. The real him with no darkness. That one had Lysander totally lost in his mind. Their eyes had met. The longing Lysander saw reflected back at him was crippling. Lysander hadn't fed in weeks. Only the magic waters of Faerie sustained him. His energy was gone. A huge part of him wanted to rush to Frost. It was possible Wulfe's town healer knew some way to free

Stone. Then again, maybe it was none of his business. Stone didn't want to see his face. So why had he been here? Lysander rolled back onto his side and curled into a ball. Knowing Stone, he had only been in his realm to fuck a different fairy. After all, he had been nude. Lysander shivered. It was always the perfect temperature where he lived. He had no idea why he was freezing.

"You look unwell."

The appearance of Stellar made Lysander smile for the first time in days. A chiseled face, carved by the gods, hovered over him. His light purple eyes flashed with concern.

"I'm okay."

A blanket appeared and covered Lysander, tucking him in and warming him. "You're not okay. I can feel your light fading. When was the last time you fed?"

Lysander's eyelids grew heavier by the second. The warmth felt nice. Darkness seemed welcoming. "I drank from the waters this morning."

Stellar nudged him. "That's not what I mean, and you know it. Don't make me forcibly read your thoughts. You know how I hate that."

Lysander bit back a sigh. Stellar was his prince. He already shouldn't be lowering himself to check on Lysander. Lysander was in no position to disobey. "I'm not sure. It's been a while."

"Why?" Stellar sounded more confused than accusing.

By his king, he didn't want to talk about this. But Stellar was not only his prince but also his oldest friend, and Lysander never knew what was a mere inquiry and what was an order.

Lysander forced his eyes open, but he still couldn't look directly at Stellar. He cleared his throat. It was an uncomfortable sound. "Apparently, a mate has been chosen for me."

Stellar gasped.

Lysander kept going. "It seems he doesn't want this match."

"What?" Stellar practically vibrated with rage. "Who is it? I'll take care of this immediately. The ridiculous idea that any fairy—"

"It's a vampire."

Stellar deflated. "I have no authority over those beasts."

Lysander couldn't look away from the changing emotions shifting over Stellar's flawless face.

After a moment, Stellar's expression landed on determined. "Scoot over. You need the power of my light."

Lysander couldn't argue. He made room for Stellar in the hammock and under the blanket.

Stellar snuggled him. Their faces were inches apart. For a while, they simply stared at each other. They had been friends for countless centuries. Time lost all meaning after a while. They knew each other so well, sometimes they didn't need to speak at all to tell each other everything.

"I think a small part of me always expected it would be us someday. Who else could possibly love us more than each other?"

The confession pulled a smile from Lysander and lightened an invisible weight on his chest. "Though it breaks my heart to admit it, I've always known there was no chance of that. You're too high above me. I never let myself dream of that future. Life would certainly be easier, though. I hate this feeling that's suffocating me, but neither can I bring myself to feed from anyone other than my mate. If my light extinguishes, I'm so grateful to have you with me."

"Absolutely not. I'm still your prince. You're not allowed to abandon me." Stellar's mouth covered his. The carnality of the kiss sang through Lysander's blood. One kiss from Stellar was hotter than any other fairy could muster within hours of the dirtiest of acts. But it was still only a kiss, and that wouldn't hold him for long.

Stellar pulled away a hair before brushing his lips across Lysander's a final time. "I know that's barely a snack, but I won't demand you to betray your mate. Give me a few hours. I'll move heaven and earth to fix this."

"Okay."

Even as Lysander agreed, he knew it was too late. The combination of starvation and mental pain was too much for his kind. They were sex and light. Lysander had lost those things. He had no idea what Stellar would do to fix what Lysander couldn't. He couldn't force Stone to want him. Lysander highly doubted Stellar could get Celeste to change her mind about her choice for him. He didn't even know how any of that worked. Celeste was the goddess who paired souls. She was the only being who knew how these decisions were made. Lysander hadn't even thought about gaining a mate. Maybe secretly, he, too, had thought he would eventually belong to Stellar. But he always dismissed those thoughts as quickly as they came. Stellar would end up with someone as powerful as he was. That was how things worked. That didn't dampen the fact that Lysander had never shared such a strong bond with anyone else. Stellar was a piece of him he couldn't live without. Lysander saw the difference now, though. This ache to be with Stone was unlike anything he had ever suffered. The pain was unimaginable.

Stellar kissed him again. "Hold on."

Lysander nodded. "I will."

Stellar vanished.

Lysander stared at the empty spot where Stellar had been. He wondered if he had just told his first and last lie to his prince.

As Stone paced Frost's home clinic, he freaked himself out a little more by the minute. Apparently, not only had Frost been back in town for a period of time Stone didn't recall, but he had also come home with a new daughter. Stone had less than zero knowledge of all this. Everyone acted as if he had shown up for every shift and the news shouldn't be a surprise. That was terrifying. What the hell had he been doing when he lost track of time? The possibilities were horrific.

A tiny baby sound came from a nearby bassinet.

Frost glanced up from the book he studied.

Stone stole the opportunity to focus on something tangible. He moved to the bassinet and looked inside. Frost and Gemini's daughter, Celina, opened her eyes for half a second before she was out again. She was the newest of newborns, and it was hard work growing. No doubt she was exhausted. Staring at her brought him peace in a way he couldn't explain. Maybe it was just the fact that she was a baby. She represented everything good and pure in the world. He was none of those things.

"She has Gemini's hair and eyes."

"No." Frost's denial had Stone's gaze snapping his way. A huge grin split Frost's face. Despite his friendly demeanor, Frost sounded firm. "I know you'll still be the same player as you are right now in twenty years, so no. My daughter is off limits."

Stone snorted and shook his head. "I can't believe you think so little of me."

Frost eyed him. "You know better than that. What's going on with you today? I know guarding me is tedious as hell, but you're not usually a pacer."

As if Frost's question triggered something inside him, Stone went back to pacing. "You have a lot on your hands right now."

Frost didn't back down. "I always have a lot on my hands. That changes nothing. If you need me, you can talk to me."

Stone glanced his way. There might not be another time. He was himself right now. Maybe he wouldn't be in an hour. Who knew if he would ever come back after that? "How do you feel about taking on a challenging case?"

"I'm always up for being tested. Give me the rundown."

Stone twisted his fingers as he walked from one side of the room to the other. His stride got longer with each pass. "What if someone was losing time with zero memory of what happened between the present and their last memory? How would you treat that?"

"Without knowing anything about the species, all I can say is, likely a series of tests would be performed. Are there any other symptoms?"

He stopped and focused on Frost. "Lethargy, dark thoughts, and randomly spacing out. I don't know."

Frost nodded. He looked as if he took the matter seriously. "How close are you to this patient?"

Gemini popped into the room, interrupting them. He headed straight for Celina. "You have company."

Before either of them could inquire, especially since Stone should have been warned of anyone on the property, a procession of people filed into the room. Tall and trim guards, with genuine gold and silver armor that accentuated their physique, carried halberds and encircled a blond—for Stone's lack of any other description—a blond god. Oddly, Deidra was fluttering around them, looking a mess.

Frost immediately came to his feet. "What's wrong, angel? Are you okay?"

Deidra ran straight to Frost. They were best friends. Stone's issues vanished. "It's my cousin. You know, Lysander. He needs help." Her panicked gaze swept the room before landing on Celina. "There's my sweet goddaughter." She swiped her hands through the air. "No. I can't hold the baby right now. Lysander needs help."

Everything inside Stone had frozen at the first mention of Lysander. He had already gathered his weapons and was ready to move.

Frost grabbed his bag and quickly kissed Celina and Gemini. "I'll be safe."

Stone gave a sharp nod at the promise, lending his reassurances. "I won't leave his side."

Gemini smiled. "Dinner will be waiting."

The blond beauty finally spoke, sounding as perfect as his form. "You're not needed. We'll be safely in Faerie with my Royal Guard's protection."

At the mention of his Royal Guard, the men surrounding him tapped their halberds on the floor.

Celina started crying.

Violet eyes turned her way. They turned to lavender as Stone watched.

Celina immediately settled.

Those unnatural eyes focused on him. “We’re wasting time.”

Stone held his ground. “Frost goes nowhere without me.” There was no denying the determination in his voice. Royalty didn’t mean shit to him. He answered only to Celeste.

The mesmerizing gaze swept over him. “Not just anyone can storm into Faerie, no matter how righteous the cause.”

Deidra patted his arm. “Stone is good, Stellar. He’s eaten food served by Jacen.”

Stone had actually forgotten that was a thing, but yeah. Frost often held backyard gatherings where Deidra's husband always manned the grill. He didn't eat any longer, but he had taken small bites of the food offered to him by Jacen for just this reason. That answered one question from his morning lapse. That was how he had seen into Faerie. Stone was more certain than ever that moment had been real. He had seen the way Lysander faded. Terror struck his heart.

"Let's go. We're wasting time."

As if Stone's reminder broke his resistance, the royal fairy, obviously named Stellar, turned away. Everyone immediately fell into step, keeping him safe from every vantage point. Stellar swept his arm, and an invisible curtain opened, giving them passage straight into Faerie.

Stone had no idea how anything worked in the hidden realm. He just stuck to Frost's back and kept his eyes moving. Despite the beauty surrounding them, bad things happened everywhere. Frost had a child and mate to go home to. It didn't take long for Lysander to come into view. A thick blanket covered his hammock suspended by nothing in midair. An unnaturally blue creek flowed beneath him. One translucent wing poked out between the hammock and blanket. Tiny shimmers of light danced on the very tip while the rest looked lifeless.

Deidra aggressively patted Frost's arm. "He's right there." It was an unnecessary announcement, but Stone got it. He felt helpless too.

Stellar motioned the hammock closer, and the bed obeyed. "I've brought the healer." Stellar reached beneath the blanket as if grabbing Lysander's hand. The love etched on the guy's face had Stone ready to fuck up that beauty. Now wasn't the time.

"He can't fix me, and you know it." There was a sad yet loving whisper from beneath the blanket. "It's okay."

Stellar snapped, "It's not okay. You've been my best friend for nearly our entire lives. If you won't live for me, at least give me a name so I can tear out his insides when you're gone."

Frost rocked from foot to foot, obviously waiting to jump in the moment he was allowed to do so. A gnawing at the back of Stone's gut and mind had him ready to explode. Everything felt wrong. There was a hole growing in his chest. More light sprinkled onto the ground like glitter from Lysander's wing. The full memory of this morning washed over him. They had locked eyes. Lysander was his mate.

"Just let me go."

"Fuck that." The roar burst from Stone. He didn't give anyone time to react. Stone used his vampire speed against the surrounding guards, bypassing them in one swift move. In a flash, he had Lysander in his arms. His mouth covered his mate's. A flash of light nearly blinded him even with his eyes closed.

Stone spoke against Lysander's lips between kisses. "You don't get to leave me like this."

"Fascinating." Frost's mutter reminded him they weren't alone. He pulled away, completely on board to do whatever it took to make Lysander live. His glowing fairy was back. No more drooping wings.

"I see." Stellar's voice had changed. He sounded less sure of himself. "You said he was a vampire. I guess I didn't know who to suspect first. Maybe I'm not as much your—" Stellar stopped. His gaze landed on Deidra. "Thank you for accompanying me. I need to get back to my place, it seems."

At any other time, maybe Stone would have tried to puzzle his way through the encounter. Right now, he still felt sick, and he didn't know why. Lysander looked better but still weak. He had no idea why everyone seemed to deem him well.

Deidra linked arms with Frost. "I'll escort you back."

Stone had never been more torn in his life. He had to guard Frost, but it was Lysander. Stone felt the way he still struggled. Which duty was he meant to follow?

Deidra made a dismissive motion when Stone tried to stand. "I'm taking him right back to his office. He's not in danger. Plus, Frost is probably more dangerous than anything bent on harming him. You stay here and fix my cousin. It seems this is your fault in the first place." The way Deidra's voice hardened had him guilt-ridden, and he had no idea what he had done.

Stone might have argued if everything hadn't felt like it wasn't real. He felt like he walked through a dream and couldn't see anything clearly, except Lysander. Only when he looked at Lysander did the world snap back into focus.

Light green eyes with rays of blue stared back at him. "I thought you said you never wanted to see my face again."

Stone got more confused every time anyone spoke to him. "I don't remember saying that, but I know that means nothing. Nothing I do lately seems to stick to my brain. Everything vanishes and I can't make my mind hang on to it, but I'm here. Please tell me what's wrong? What's happening to your wings?"

At his question, Lysander's wings disappeared as if he didn't want Stone to see them. "I haven't truly fed in weeks."

That one threw Stone for all the loops. "So eat."

A soft, weak-sounding chuckle vibrated from Lysander. Even at death's door, the laugh sounded sexual. Lysander was just pure lust. The truth dawned. He felt a little dumb. "Oh. Why won't you do what you need to do? I know it's not from lack of offers." Even as Stone said the words, a jealous rage roared through him. No one else was allowed to touch his mate. He knew the reaction wasn't fair. If Lysander forbade him from drinking from anyone else, he wouldn't understand. Blood was food. That was all. For Lysander, sex was magic, light, and energy. Truthfully, fairies were akin to energy vampires. Stone should be looking at this as he would any other food source, but he couldn't. This was his mate.

Lysander's gaze moved over Stone's face, as if looking to see if Stone would get smarter. When he came to the obvious conclusion that Stone would never figure him out, he put Stone out of his misery. "I don't want to touch anyone else. It wouldn't be right."

Stone hated how that confession simultaneously made his heart soar and sink. He ached to claim his mate—to be claimed by his mate. But Stone had a sickness he didn't know if he could spread. Neither could he fail this beautiful gift from Celeste. A fairy. Stone nearly laughed. He couldn't say she hadn't matched his appetite.

Still, Stone wanted to protect Lysander. "Maybe it wouldn't be right if I touched you."

Lysander nodded as if he saw every thought and fear inside Stone. "Then I'll touch you."

Lysander's fingertips ran down Stone's torso. His shirt disappeared beneath Lysander's touch. Stone stared so hard at Lysander, his vision doubled, forcing him to blink. He had to stay in this moment. They had so much to talk about, but Stone didn't know how long he had before his mind wasn't his any longer. No matter what, he couldn't let Lysander starve because of him. Nor could he force himself to give Lysander permission to go somewhere else.

While holding Lysander's gaze, Stone kept his voice serious. "You know hammock sex is hard, right?"

The hammock dropped, turning into a bed before hitting the ground. He was almost bucked off the edge at the impact. Stone wasn't one to let something like being graceless stop him from getting what he wanted.

He straddled Lysander's body. "Now do the pants." Now that he had Lysander where he wanted him, he felt more like himself than he had in months.

Lysander touched Stone's hip, and his jeans disappeared. He glanced behind him. His work boots were still firmly in place. "That's how it's gonna be, huh?"

A mischievous smile stretched across Lysander's face. Not even his weakened state dimmed his carnality, which practically dripped from him. "When you're about to work, you need the proper equipment."

Happiness rushed through him, the way it had always done when Stone found himself alone with Lysander. Goddess, he couldn't have asked for a better pairing. If he had to spend eternity with anyone, he was glad it was Lysander. He always made every thought and worry vanish.

Lysander stroked Stone's erection. His skin tone improved by the second. "I'm already wet for you. You should take advantage of that."

Fuck, he was hot. Lysander's brand of magic made everything better. He never had to stop to find lube. Still... "You're my mate. I want better for you than just to get fucked."

Their connection grew closer at his admission. He felt the pride rise inside Lysander. Lysander needed Stone to recognize their bond. The knowledge came as clearly as if those thoughts had been his own.

"Considering I might actually die if you don't get inside me soon, I'm pretty cool with just getting fucked. Plus, I love the—"

Lysander's words were cut short by his cry as Stone quickly changed positions and impaled him. A bright glow radiated from his body, and his back bowed. Yeah. This was his person. Stone went wild. Lysander's hole was like nothing he had ever experienced elsewhere, and Stone was a self-proclaimed man-whore. He had enjoyed centuries of every creature in existence. In retrospect, he should have recognized Lysander as his mate immediately. Stone had been told his entire life that mates were different. That no one else would quench his thirst after their coupling. He believed it, since he hadn't—willingly—wanted anyone else since. Stone had to slam the door on those thoughts. He didn't know how much Lysander could see in his mind yet. The last thing he wanted was for Lysander to get hurt. Plus, Lysander felt fucking amazing beneath him. Stone wanted to remember every second.

His fangs scraped Lysander's skin. He was scared to bite. Stone wasn't so far gone that he had forgotten he was sick. He couldn't harm his mate.

Lysander didn't give him a choice in the matter. He snatched Stone's hair and dragged him into a kiss. Before Stone saw it coming, he had Stone's neck in his mouth with another swift tug. Blinding lights popped in his vision as Lysander's teeth sank into his skin. If Stone had been the least bit capable, he would have begged Lysander to stop. He would tell Lysander everything and ensure he understood why this was a bad idea. Nothing but blinding ecstasy existed in his mind and body. He couldn't even move from the way his cock pumped jets of cum into Lysander's ass. Stone couldn't come down. The mind-bending orgasm seemed to last forever. Someone could walk right up and kill him. Stone still wouldn't know he was dead. He couldn't even breathe. His hips wouldn't stop rolling, trying to get as deep as possible. Lysander licked the place he had bitten, and Stone's mind cleared a little. A gust of wind chilled the cum coating Stone's torso. That was the only proof he had that he'd pleased Lysander. At least he hadn't totally failed Lysander... yet.

"You won't destroy me. I feel how badly you want this. The longing coats your mind. It's all I can see."

Lysander had claimed him, and now he saw the ugliness. Damn. Lysander had claimed him. This time, that thought fully sank in. Lysander was right. The longing crippled him. His fangs itched to bite—to take his rightful place.

“Please? I want that.”

At Lysander’s plea, Stone kissed his neck, equally teasing them. His body tingled with anticipation. He might come again. It would be just explosive. Stone was sure of it. He was still hard inside Lysander, ready to make him leak with cum for days. He sucked the spot he had kissed. His hunger grew bigger than anything he had ever experienced. Stone swore he already tasted the magic-filled blood coating his mouth.

Nope. Not today, slave. A claimed mate will give you grounding I can't tolerate right now. I'm not done with you yet.

"No." Stone didn't know if the guttural denial was Lysander's or his.

He couldn't even see Lysander any longer, much less feel him. Everything surrounding him was just gone. He fought like hell to find the light. Any light. Nothing existed but an inky void.

For fuck's sake. Stop fighting. You'll get your pathetic mate back soon enough.

"Let me go." Stone screamed the words and pushed as hard as he could against the walls of his mind. For a moment, he stood feet from Lysander. Lysander looked terrified. Fear filled every inch of Stone. "What's happening to me?"

Stone would never know if Lysander answered. Things went black again. This time, he was gone.

Chapter Three

THERE WAS NO TIME to waste. Lysander was recharged. He had claimed his mate, and now he saw everything Stone did. While Lysander might be just a fairy to other creatures, their species shouldn't be overlooked. The magic they wove through the world was a powerful thing. He wasn't afraid to fight. Lysander had once been a soldier for his people. He could be that warrior again.

Lysander dressed as a human would before appearing at Frost's door. Alarms blared, and vampires appeared, surrounding him. They looked fierce and ready to kill any enemy. Lysander did his best to remain as sultry as possible. Nothing disarmed men like lust.

Leif was the first to lower his sword. "Lysander, hey." He eyed Lysander for a moment. "You don't look sick to me."

"I'm well."

The deep line between Leif's eyebrows didn't relax. "I thought Stone was with you."

Before Lysander could speak, the front door opened. Stone stared out at him. "I take it the perimeter alarm was a false one."

His eyes were different. Even Leif looked confused by him. He wasn't Stone. Things were worse than Lysander feared. The dark one obviously lived Stone's life like nothing had changed. Was this a ploy to get close to Frost? Would he hurt Celina? Lysander couldn't let that happen.

"I thought you were still in Faerie."

Stone shrugged at Leif's statement. "I got back a few minutes ago." His gaze latched onto Lysander. "I assume you're here for Frost."

Lysander nodded along, keeping the lie going. "I—"

"Lysander! Come in. You're on your feet." Frost's timely appearance saved him. Lysander had a feeling Stone's hijacker planned to find a way to turn him away.

Lysander passed Stone as if they barely knew each other and walked with Frost back to the clinic section of his home. "Yeah, I thought maybe I should get the once-over to make sure there's no lingering damage." *Can you hear me?*

Thankfully, Frost seemed accustomed to having his mind steamrolled. "Yeah." He dragged out the word, as if signaling he responded to the spoken statement and the mental inquiry. "We should definitely do that. You were frighteningly close to passing into the next life."

He felt Stone on their heels, listening to every word. "I've never gotten that bad before. I still feel a little queasy." *Don't react. Stone is currently possessed.*

"This is new territory for me, but I appreciate the chance to study this phenomenon. I find fairies fascinating." *What do we do? Should I alert the other guards?*

Play this calmly. "I'm always up for being used in the name of science." Lysander threw as much sexual innuendo as he could behind the claim. He couldn't let Stone suspect anything.

Frost motioned for Stone to stay put as they reached the door of the clinic. "Doctor, patient privacy and all that. I'll have to ask you to wait here."

Stone's eyes flickered Lysander's way. "Of course."

Lysander didn't breathe too much in relief when the door closed between them. He knew Stone would still hear every word.

"Just let me grab my stethoscope. I need you to take some deep breaths for me." Frost pretended to listen to his heart and lungs. *Tell me.* "Just breathe in and out."

His mind is hijacked by a dark fae, making him extremely dangerous. I don't think the dark one always has control, though. You can tell by his eyes. They're not his eyes. I can see inside his mind and see the beast behind the mask. I don't know why this is happening or what the fae seeks. But I need you to help me fix him.

Frost froze. "Your heart and lungs sound fine." *How can I help?*

Lysander paced away. Celina was awake in her bassinet, chewing her hands. She would be stunning one day. *Where is Gemini?*

“Your pulse seems strong too. I’d like to get some bloodwork.” *I told him to take a nap. He was up with Celina all night.*

Lysander smiled. His eyes returned to the baby he hovered over. “She’s such a good baby. Quiet.” *She might also be in danger. I don’t know, but Gemini should take her away from this place.*

Frost’s eyes flashed in a way Lysander had never seen before. *I’m the most dangerous being in this house. No one will harm her.* Power practically radiated from Frost.

Just the same. I think it’ll take both of us to pull this beast from Stone. Please. I want my mate back.

Sympathy crossed Frost's features. *I've asked Gemini to get Leif. Then he'll come for Celina. We have a plan.*

Lysander nodded. "It's odd to see such a small human, but she's beautiful."

"Do they have babies in Faerie? I've never thought to ask, but now that I think about it, I can't recall ever seeing a single fairy child."

Lysander chuckled. He couldn't help the lust-filled tinge to the sound. "Faerie isn't a child-friendly realm. Every day there is a sexual feast. To answer your question, though, no. Fairies are born from magic fully formed and return to pure magic when we die."

"Huh." Frost sounded unnervingly calm for the situation they were in.

"That's fascinating as hell. How do you define families, then? Deidra is your cousin, and there's a royal family."

Lysander wished he could think clearly. Inside, he was a mess. "There're different lineages of magic. It's not all equal. Most enchantments are born from nature, like the air and the trees. I was born of water. Our king—"

A soft knock interrupted them.

Frost didn't hesitate. "Come in."

Gemini poked his head inside. "Is it safe?"

Lysander laughed. "Don't worry. I'm dressed, but my natural form is so much better." He couldn't let Stone suspect him of being anything other than himself.

Gemini stepped fully inside the room. He had Stone and Leif on his heels. Leif closed the door behind them. On the sly, he touched the door. Since Leif was a Druid vampire, Lysander assumed he used his magic to secure the room.

Gemini picked up Celina. He kissed Frost. "Grandpa is demanding time with his granddaughter."

Frost gave him a sharp nod. "We can't have him missing his grandbaby."

Lysander assumed Frost understood Gemini's code.

The room seemed to hold its breath as Gemini headed to a room Lysander suspected was Frost's office.

Frost focused on Stone. A kind and professional smile sat sturdy on his features. "I haven't thought to ask how you are this morning. It's not every day you meet your mate." *Wrap your arms around him. I'll need you to hold him.*

Stone didn't look suspicious. That was good. "I'm fine." He sounded completely unmoved. Zero personality. No care for Lysander's existence.

Lysander molded against Stone's back and wrapped his arms around Stone's waist. He kissed Stone's shoulder. His throat swelled. There was only a black hole where Stone should be. He forced a chuckle. "Yeah, he is." Lysander's voice dripped with sex. *I'm ready.*

Frost moved closer.

Without warning, the room turned so dark and oppressive that a chill ran through Lysander. Lysander immediately braced for a fight. He could smell the evil in the air. Then Lucifer walked into the room from the same room where Gemini had disappeared. Lysander nearly failed Stone. His knees weakened. Lysander was born of light magic. This was the actual dark one. Oddly, he was also the most beautiful man Lysander had ever set eyes on. That was what gave him strength to squeeze Stone against him. He could pretend he wasn't in the presence of pure evil. No one else seemed the least bit surprised or scared. Eyes that looked exactly like a summertime sky at noon flashed with irritation as he crossed the room. "You're interrupting my Papaw time. No one takes me away from granddaughter." That was all the warning they had before Lucifer's glowing hands reached inside Stone like dipping his hands into water. The scream that roared from Stone was the most pain-filled sound Lysander had ever heard in his life.

As quickly and easily as plucking a tissue from a tissue box, Lucifer held a human-shaped shadow. "Ah. There you are, my little spellcaster. Tell me why you cursed my son."

An evil laugh vibrated from the darkness. "You'll have nothing from me."

Lysander had no fucking clue what Lucifer meant. All he knew was the darkness was gone from Stone.

Lucifer pulled him forward, going nose to nose with the phantom form, as if he saw something no one else could. A terrifying smile spread across Lucifer's deceptively beautiful face. "I see." Lucifer snorted. "Return to Bodhi. I want him to feel the crushing blow of knowing my family is united now. He failed." During the speech, Lucifer had sounded almost normal. But at the name Bodhi, Frost gasped. Lucifer's voice hardened as his grip tightened on the nearly translucent shadow. "And if he ever comes for one of mine again, there'll be nothing left of him to be reborn. I will not play this game with you again." With a solid shake, Stone's hijacker vanished.

Lucifer sighed. The sound was a tired one. "Ridiculous." His gaze found Frost, as if no one else existed. "Come with me."

Frost didn't hesitate.

Until the choking oppression disappeared, Lysander's mind didn't clear enough for him to remember he held Stone's slumped body. A shot of panic hit him before he realized Stone was alive. He was just unconscious.

Leif rushed to help as Lysander moved Stone into the lone hospital bed. "What can I do to help? I know your magic is stronger than mine, but I can lend a hand."

For a moment, Lysander simply stared at Leif. Leif should hate him. He had once tried to win Leif's mate just to prove to himself Stone had no hold over him. Now the vamp offered his magic. That was the highest compliment among his kind.

"Thank you." Lysander sounded as sincere as he was. "He needs to be warded against possession. Stone is vulnerable now. Once one being finds its way in, a trail is left to follow for others."

Leif didn't hesitate. He waved a hand over Stone, covering his body in symbols that sank into Stone's skin and disappeared. "That should block all pathways. We should probably keep him knocked out for a bit. What do you think?"

Lysander eyed Stone inside and out. "Agreed. There's damage left behind. Wisps of darkness. We should keep him asleep until Frost gives us the all clear."

Their gazes met. A silent message passed between them. There was something big going on in this town, and they were the only two under this roof who didn't know what.

Voices chatted from all around him. Stone felt like he was in a wind tunnel. Once, when he had been much younger, he had been trapped in a snowstorm. The wind and snow had made it nearly impossible to push forward. Screams of his warrior brethren had echoed all around him, but he couldn't see anything but an eerie white. He couldn't help them. That was how he felt now. He knew people were near, but he couldn't find them. Stone had been rendered useless.

"So help me understand this. Bodhi was your great aunt, but now he's some twenty-something dude. He's out there cursing people, and it's because you're Lucifer's son." Lysander sounded confused.

"He used me to curse Frost." The words sounded like a car driving over gravel. They hurt too, but Stone knew this one. He had to warn them before the darkness returned. "Bodhi wanted you to doubt yourself so much, you left this place before Lucifer learned the truth. He used me to get close to you."

"You're awake. I thought Leif and I had done enough to keep you out for a while. You need to rest." Stone recognized Lysander's voice, but he couldn't get to him. He couldn't see a thing.

"Can't. There's too much danger. He'll be back. The darkness is always back." Stone heard himself fading. He fought the magic being used against him. "No. I need..."

For a moment, there was nothing. The snow turned into an inky field. A bright light cut through the darkness, nearly blinding Stone. Then Lysander was there. His heart rate slowed. Lysander was here. He wasn't alone. The gaping hole in his chest sealed a little as Lysander reached for him.

"Come with me." A bed came into view. It was the only thing other than them in the darkness. "I know you're scared." Lysander crawled into bed, urging Stone to join him. "But your body needs rest. I'll stay with you. You're warded now. No one can harm you."

Stone automatically obeyed Lysander's every command. The moment he was settled under the blankets, Lysander used his chest as a pillow and draped his leg over Stone's. "How are you here?" Lysander felt so real.

"I claimed you. No spell could keep me from your mind. You're my other half."

"But you're really here?" Stone couldn't stop questioning things. Too much had happened lately. He couldn't tell the difference between what was reality and what wasn't.

"I'm a fairy, baby. Maybe that makes me soft in some ways, but my spine is steel and my magic is strong. There are different layers to reality, but for all intents and purposes, I'm here every bit as much as you are. Together in our minds."

Stone held Lysander tighter. "I'm so sorry about everything. You should probably hate me by now. Even though I don't know what happened when that thing had me in its grasp, I'm sure it was terrible. Sometimes I'd wake up, and he was gone and—"

"Shhh." Lysander petted and soothed him, cutting him off. "Set it aside for now. Focus on healing."

"You should hate me," Stone repeated, sounding every bit as heartbroken as he was. Lysander had claimed him. He had to be disappointed as hell to have ended up with Stone. They both knew he was nothing more than an empty-headed flirt. For months now, he had felt nothing except rage... unless he was with Lysander. Still, all he had shown Lysander was nothing at all. How sad. He deserved so much better than Stone.

Lysander kissed his neck.

Stone closed his eyes and savored the sensation. The night they met stood out so vividly in his mind compared to recent months. He had been untainted by darkness. Lysander had been such a sexy glow cutting through the night. Life had looked so different.

The grass rustled beneath his feet. He had left his boots next to a tree at the edge of the forest. His kilt moved slightly in the wind, reminding him of bygone days. Stone closed his eyes and dragged the night air into his lungs. It smelled like freedom and something else.

Stone's eyes shot open. His entire body went on alert. Stone couldn't place the smell. It was almost tropical, which made no sense for the area. His feet carried him toward the scent. A soft light cast a glow on the nearby trees. Stone's gaze moved in every direction, searching for the source. He was in hunter mode. His chin shot up as a sound rustled above. A man sat on a tree branch. It was an odd sight. He seemed tall and looked solid, yet the narrow branch didn't even droop from his weight. His eyes were arresting. They glowed and were almost two colors, with a vivid green slowly turning to light blue around his pupils.

"Who are you?"

Stone blinked at the guy's tone. He sounded like Stone trespassed. Maybe he had. "Stone." A wicked smile stretched across Stone's lips. "I bet you have a sexy name. One that sounds amazing when moaned."

The sexiest smile Stone had ever seen in his life exploded across the man's face. "You should find out."

The way Stone felt in that moment should have given an inkling about their bond. While Stone had zero reservations about hopping from every bed he could, something about Lysander had been different. Stone had actually felt happy that night, making him realize exactly what made him jump from partner to partner. He hadn't been satisfied because no one else was Lysander.

"Sleep." The quietly spoken order enchanted Stone's mind, hypnotizing him. He could truly rest now. His mate had him.

Chapter Four

SOMETHING FAMILIAR TICKLED HIS senses. Stone snuggled deeper beneath the pillows. He was too sleepy to be curious. Stone rearranged his pillows and curled around the plush cushion. Wait. It was his pillow. He shot upright. His gaze swung from side to side. Stone's heart tried climbing into his throat. It had happened again. He was in a different place than where he had fallen asleep. What had he done this time? He wanted to puke. Stone had really thought he had gotten free this time. Had his hijacker found a new way to torment him? Would he spend the rest of his life trapped between nothing and hallucinations?

Lysander rushed into the room, holding a mug. “Oh no. I only left for five minutes to make tea. Why are you awake?”

Stone breathed as if he had barely survived running a mile. Sweat coated his skin. “I was at Frost’s. Wasn’t I? What did I do?”

Lysander set his cup on the nightstand. He sat on the edge of the bed at Stone’s hip, facing him. His eyes held Stone captive, slowing his heart. “I brought you home. All you’ve done is sleep, exactly like you needed to do. I knew you’d be more comfortable here.”

Relief had Stone falling back onto his pillows. "Thank Goddess." With the terror ebbing, his focus turned to Lysander. He wore a white silk robe, looking entirely too sexy. Stone fiddled with the material, enjoying the sensation of the loose belt running between his fingers. "Look at you, being way too tempting."

Lysander's mouth lifted at one corner. "You haven't been awake even five minutes, and I'm literally just existing at the moment."

Stone turned serious. "That's all you need to do. You have nae idea how much I hate knowing you've gotten so little of the real me."

"I haven't heard you use that thick of an accent in a while. Maybe that should've clued me in sooner that something was wrong." His expression turned sad. "I'm sorry I failed you."

There was a hollow spot in his chest. Stone ran his hand up Lysander's thigh. "No. I—" Stone swallowed. The longer they sat there, enjoying each other's space, the more it sank in that this was his mate. Lysander had claimed him. No doubt, that hadn't been an easy decision for him, considering Stone's drama. Yet he hadn't hesitated, and Stone hadn't given him the same courtesy. He had heard it was painful to go unclaimed. Lysander had grace in a way Stone had never witnessed. He hadn't complained or asked to be put out of his misery. In fact, he had been ready to return to magic rather than inconvenience him. Stone hated he felt that way. Without claiming Lysander, he couldn't see into his mind. Stone had never understood that one. As a vampire, he should hear every thought Lysander had. There was nothing. With no way of checking his emotions, Stone felt worse by the second. Why had Lysander been so willing to pass to another existence rather than come to Stone?

A terrible feeling rose in his gut. He searched the recesses of his mind, frantically fighting to learn what he had done while possessed.

Lysander brushed a sweet kiss across his lips. "Don't do this to yourself."

Damn. He was Lysander's mate. He could look into Stone's mind anytime he liked. It was his right. "Please tell me what I did."

"Only because it's important to you and you seem to keep forgetting about it." He sighed and righted himself. "You told me you never wanted to see my face ever again. I guess I overreacted a little."

Stone's eyes fell closed. That fae fucker had done his best to level Stone's life. He didn't even know how he had ended up possessed. Months were just gone, and it was maddening. Stone forced himself to focus on Lysander. His mate deserved for him to face this head-on. "You're my mate. I imagine I'd feel the same if you rejected me. But I hope you know I would never treat you that way. It wasn't me."

A sweet smile crossed Lysander's lips. "You're a lover first and then a warrior. Logically, I knew it wasn't you. While you had me pinned against the tree, I saw your eyes."

"Hold up. I had you pinned against a tree. Did I hurt you?" Please, Goddess. He couldn't know he had hurt Lysander.

"Just my feelings." His serene smile didn't waver. "Tell me what I can do for you."

Stone smirked. He didn't even think about it. It was such second nature when he was with Lysander. He made the world and all Stone's problems vanish with a single question.

A smile exploded across Lysander's sexy face. "There you are."

Stone felt stronger by the minute. His fangs itched. There was a hunger growing bigger inside him the more he sat with Lysander. The need to claim his mate drowned out everything else. With a light tug, he had Lysander's robe falling open. His gaze slid down Lysander's flawless body. His light brown skin glistened with a hint of glitter.

With the sight of Lysander's body hypnotizing him, Stone's thoughts turned into words. "I've never met anyone sexier. You captivated me the moment I looked up into that tree. My little dewdrop, precariously balanced on a branch. All I had to do was raise my arms, and you were in my grasp." He held Lysander's stare. "You're mine. I want more."

Lysander straddled his body. "Take what you need."

In one swift motion, Stone had Lysander beneath him. Not only was Lysander light as a feather, Stone was a vampire. Lysander didn't stand a chance against his strength.

"Maybe, but..." Lysander vanished from beneath him and reappeared straddling his back. Stone's breath quickened. He buried his face in the mattress. His dick already wept. It was obvious Lysander was in his head. Stone loved it. "... I can make you wet."

Stone felt the tingle of magic dancing on his asshole. He moaned and leaned into the sensation. Fuck. The curse dragged out inside his mind. There was no one like his mate.

Lysander urged Stone to move his knees. He spread Stone's ass cheeks. "Yeah. That's what I want."

Stone wondered if he would come from Lysander's words alone. Then Lysander thrust inside him and Stone begged.

"Please? Fuck. I need—" His words died on a strangled cry as Lysander dragged his upper body upward and against his chest, forcing Stone to cling to the top of the headboard to brace himself. The way he moved inside Stone was mesmerizing. His body moved beautifully against him. The moment Lysander's forearm encircled his throat, Stone broke. He grabbed Lysander's arm and bit. His heart refused to go another second without joining its other half. Satisfaction roared through him when the sensation of being stitched to Lysander filled his chest. His dick bounced with every hard thrust. Cum shot from him, painting the mattress and his pillow. The sounds that he made as they shared an orgasm would likely leave an imprint on his brain. There was ecstasy, and then there was this powerful satisfaction that had no name. Reality ceased to exist, yet life felt realer. Then Lysander's teeth sank into his shoulder. Stone blacked out for a moment. He had never put much stock in finding his true mate. His life had never felt empty. But, dear Goddess, how had he survived without this beautiful thing between them? Stone already knew he would die without it.

Same.

Lysander kept his eyes closed, savoring the sensation of Stone counting each bump of his spine. Steam rose from the water surrounding them.

"You always smell exactly like this place: tropical and irresistible."

Lysander smiled. Contentment filled him. The hot springs in Faerie hadn't felt this welcoming in years. He wondered if everything would feel new again when he shared the experience with Stone.

"You smell like Scotland: wild."

A sexy-sounding chuckle rumbled behind him. "Wild doesn't sound good. In my experience, wild creatures stink."

Lysander couldn't stop smiling as he leaned back against Stone's chest. "I'm a fairy, born from nature. You smell amazing. Not the least bit stinky." Lysander chuckled as he added the last.

The air turned serious. Stone's arms wrapped around him, gently holding him. "How do fairy folk feel about vampires?"

Stone's worry was right there for Lysander to inspect. "Fairies don't discriminate. If it's fuckable, then it's fair game." He laughed. "Within reason, of course."

"Of course." The heavy laughter in Stone's voice kept Lysander smiling. Then he felt Stone's trepidation rise. Lysander couldn't stop himself from scraping Stone's mind. His shoulders relaxed. Stone had nothing to worry about. Lysander could easily put all his worries at ease.

"I mostly survive on honeysuckle juice. Sometimes, I still enjoy the full-meal experience. You don't have to worry about starving me by admitting you don't want me to turn to anyone else for the sexual energy I need to survive. I'm old. I can go months without feeding."

That seemed to catch Stone's attention. "Months? You were on the edge of death just a few days ago."

He knew Stone could reach inside his mind and take the answers he sought. Lysander wasn't sure why he didn't choose to do so. The memories and his feelings attached were right there for the taking.

The Scot was a gorgeous sight roaming through the woods. The Weres' midnight run took place a few miles away. Lysander didn't know why Stone hadn't joined in tonight. From his observations from afar, Stone never held back if he got a chance at someone's bed.

Stone moved closer to Lysander's hiding spot. From his experience, anytime anyone wanted to hide, the trees were the place to be. No one ever looked up. Making a liar of him, Stone focused on him like he had known exactly where Lysander had been hiding all along.

Lysander panicked a little. He didn't want Stone to think he had been stalking him, even though he had. Fairies could rarely resist the scent of a sexual being like Stone. "Who are you?" There. It was like they had truly happened upon each other.

Stone blinked, as if Lysander's question caught him off guard. "Stone." The wickedest smile Lysander had ever seen stretched Stone's lips. "I bet you have a sexy name. One that sounds amazing when moaned."

A smile exploded across Lysander's face. "You should find out." He near-

ly cackled at Stone's expression. The vamp had not seen that one coming, apparently.

Stone quickly rallied, making Lysander proud. He held his arms up. "I'll catch you."

Lysander knew he would, but Lysander believed in full transparency. His wings unfurled and gently lowered him into Stone's hold.

Stone smirked. "That was hot."

Something stirred inside Lysander he hadn't felt in years, real lust. Not just the need to energize himself, but pure desire and hunger. He would embrace it.

"I guess after I ran into a sexy Scot in the middle of the night, I didn't want anyone else."

"Holy shit, Lysander. That *was* months ago. I know I was kind of out of it the other day when you were slipping away and didn't firmly grasp a thing, but fuck. You never should've gone that long without feeding."

A smile tugged at Lysander's lips at Stone's outrage. "At first, I had no plans to do so. Then we kept running into each other, and you infuriated me like no one ever has. But I couldn't stop craving you, and I didn't know why, and that pissed me off even more." He shrugged. "I suppose I was obsessed."

"We kept running into each other?"

Damn. It seemed they hadn't. "I'm guessing you were possessed the entire time."

Stone's lips skimmed Lysander's neck, making his breathing shaky. "Not the night we met. I was there for every earthshaking moment of that. Since then, it's just the scattered and broken memory here and there."

Lysander was torn between giving in to temptation and curiosity. "What's the last clear memory you have?" Maybe they could retrace Stone's steps.

He saw Stone flipping through the visions in his head, searching for the answer. "Walking through the woods the morning after we met. I didn't want to leave, but it was time for my shift at Frost's. My every thought was still with you. I don't remember seeing any threats. All I could think about was how good you tasted, and I was dying to know how sweet your blood would be. I was plotting ways to see you again, and that never happens to me. Then Frost's cabin came into view from the woods, and then nothing." Stone held his silence. His frustration was crushing Lysander's chest. "What have I been doing this entire time? It could've been anything."

"I don't know." Lysander spoke the words quietly. Stone's story cleared up nothing. All he had now was more questions. One of their run-ins had been at Aspen's house. Lysander had flirted heavily with the bear and even had a date planned. When he had shown up, Stone had already been there. He had acted suspicious when he saw Lysander. At the time, Lysander thought Aspen was another of Stone's conquests, and they had a heated argument. The memory deepened his confusion.

“Do you remember seeing me at Aspen’s place?”

“Aspen has a place in Wulfe?”

Damn, he really had missed a lot. “Yes. He’s Leif’s mate. That’s beside the point, though. We fought that night. When I showed up on his doorstep, you were there. We equally accused each other of sleeping with Aspen.”

“Why?” Stone sounded confused to the point of anger.

Lysander waved the question away. “It doesn’t matter now. The point is, you genuinely fought with me—ugly jealousy and all. Why would this entity do that? He could’ve just walked away from me and not engaged. Why hold that argument?"

He could practically hear the wheels turning in Stone's head. Finally, he sighed. "I guess we'll never know now. What did I say I was doing at Aspen's place?"

Lysander shrugged. "You refused to tell me. You just kept repeating it was business. Obviously, that was so outlandish, I didn't believe you. We should question some people. Maybe we can figure this mess out."

Stone kissed his shoulder. "Is it okay if we don't focus on this anymore today?"

Lysander got it. They were newly mated. It was supposed to be their time to savor the blessing they had been handed.

I'm glad it's you.

A smile touched Lysander's lips as the words brushed his mind. "I'll make you happy."

He felt Stone smile against his shoulder. "Not even a concern of mine." His hand slid down Lysander's stomach. "I'll make us both happy."

Oh, Lysander knew that. He was already ecstatic.

With his gaze locked on the corner of the room, Frost ran through every second he had spent with Stone since he reopened the doors to his practice. He found it hard to believe Stone had been possessed the entire time. The guy had been right there, inches from Celina a dozen times. Anything could have happened. Obviously, Frost would have shredded him to pieces. But Stone could have killed her before Frost saw it coming. His heart couldn't handle even the thought of it.

"I think the three of you should move here."

At the suggestion, Frost tore his gaze away from the hole he stared into the wall. "What?"

Lucifer paced with Celina asleep on his shoulder. "My grandbaby isn't safe with Bodhi on the loose. I should've known he would be back one day, especially since I found you. We need to be proactive. You should live here."

He had too many thoughts to name. "You think the woman who raised me would hurt Celina?"

"We're not raising our daughter in Hell," Gemini said at the same time.

Lucifer rolled his eyes at Gemini. "You can't possibly think I wouldn't create a little paradise here for her. Nothing about your home would remotely seem like Hell. Plus, you're here now. I know you don't think you'll stop bringing her here as she ages." The dark note in Lucifer's tone said that they would never keep Celina from him.

Frost interceded. "Of course, she'll always be available for you. You're her Papaw. She adores you, and you're my dad. I feel the same."

Lucifer sniffed but seemed mollified.

Frost pressed on. "Gemini just means she shouldn't have to hide. We shouldn't have to keep her from the sunshine and fresh air. She's half snow leopard. Being trapped will eventually go against her nature. Plus, we shouldn't have to live in fucking fear all the time. This is ridiculous."

Lucifer sat. His gaze never wavered from Frost. "You're my son. I would never allow harm to come to your family.

To answer your question, I doubt Bodhi would physically hurt you. But he's already cursed you once, and Gemini could be next... or Celina. Maybe he'll see her as an abomination he needs to destroy."

Fuck. He got it, but he really didn't want to live in Hell. He had a practice and a family. A life.

Lucifer's shoulders slumped as if he listened to Frost's thoughts. A bassinet appeared at his side. Lucifer gently put Celina down so she wouldn't wake. Immediately, Yuri and Brownie flanked her and rested their big canine heads on the edge of the bed. The way they stared at her had Frost's heart overflowing with love. Celina was well guarded here. Well loved here. He couldn't make this decision.

"Has Celeste met her yet?"

The quietly spoken question dragged his attention back to his dad. "No. It's not that I'm still angry or anything. I don't know why, honestly."

Lucifer's serious tone never wavered. "You should call out to her. If you can't raise Celina here, let Celeste help protect her. I'd offer a demon to guard her, but I know you'd never accept. You'll probably feel more comfortable with an angel."

We're hurting him.

Gemini sent the mental message at the same moment he had a similar thought. Frost didn't know how to handle this. *I want us on the same page.*

He felt Gemini's support before he even responded. *I trust you. In retrospect, he created Celina. He loves her. That's massive. He'd never let her be harmed, but there is someone out there who might feel differently. He's right: your aunt or not, she might see Celina as something she can't allow to live.*

Unfortunately, Frost had already had that worry in the back of mind before anyone else had spoken it. Gemini's and Lucifer's words meant Frost wasn't just needlessly worried. His aunt had been reborn. He didn't know her anymore. It seemed she was a man now. Frost wouldn't see her coming. Bodhi could be anyone.

"I suppose this would allow me to convert the entire cabin into a clinic and have a few more private rooms for patients. I could deliver babies there in a controlled environment."

Lucifer looked flabbergasted and afraid to hope. "I could do that for you in a snap."

"Maybe you should teach Frost how to do it himself in a snap. That's a skill he'll need if he intends to live here." Riku had been so quiet, sitting in the corner with a book, Frost had forgotten he was there.

Frost had to slow things down. "Wait. I haven't agreed to anything yet. There's no way for patients to contact me here. I'm grateful you created a new mirror for us, so I wouldn't have to fall through the ceiling with Celina, but I understand that's a risk. Celina isn't any better protected if people can pour in to seek help."

Lucifer waved off his concerns. "I already have a few ideas to ensure your place in Wulfe isn't affected. If you hadn't been called to help, I never would've found you. That oddly matters to me."

A bark of laughter burst from Frost at the droll words. Now he sounded like Lucifer. He glanced Gemini's way. Gemini held his stare. Neither of them wanted this, but Celina had to come first. They would make it work.

Chapter Five

IT WASN'T ALL IN his head. Everyone acted weird around him. When Stone had appeared for his shift, he had assumed word had already spread about his possession. Stone didn't know what he had expected, but the side eye and open pity hadn't made the list. Stone wasn't one to fade into the background, but he still didn't feel like himself. Their reactions sent him scrambling inside to Frost. He didn't stop to chat. It was his job to hover over the sexy doctor all day. Plus, he kind of looked forward to seeing Celina. Now that he knew he wouldn't transform into something horrible at any second, he wondered if Frost would let him hold her. She truly was adorable.

The moment Stone stepped inside the cabin, he froze. Nothing looked the same. Stone stepped back out onto the screened-in front porch, ensured he was definitely at the right place, and then stepped back inside again. While the outside of the cabin was unchanged, the inside had completely transformed. It looked like a miniature hospital. Complete with a grumpy-looking front desk worker, and all. The guy eyed Stone with heavy suspicion. “What do you want?”

The snapped question stiffened Stone’s spine. Before he could respond, a tall, slender, and dark-haired man walked into the room. A chuckle that sent chills racing down Stone's body rumbled through the air.

"Now, now, Mordred. We've talked about this. You can't greet patients like that."

Mordred sneered.

"I'm not a patient."

The new arrival's glowing blue eyes focused on Stone. Every warning bell he possessed rang. He smelled smoke and brimstone. "My apologies. How may we help you?"

The warrior in Stone wanted to pounce. It was his job to keep Frost safe. This creature screamed danger. "I'm Frost's guard for the day."

The unnatural blue gaze swept down Stone's body. "Lucky him. I'm Desir, his new office manager. Come this way."

Stone followed as Desir led him down a hallway that hadn't existed the last time Stone had been here. He eyed the unusual entity. A dawning suspicion grew as unwanted desire filled the air. Stone blinked. That was it. He was a lust demon.

Frost and Celina came into sight. Before he could act on his recognition, Desir headed for Celina.

Stone nearly tripped trying to get to her to stop him. "No. Don't let him touch the baby. A demon's touch is poison." Stone's shout startled Celina. Her cries filled the air.

Desir shot him look, letting Stone know exactly who he blamed.

Frost looked baffled. “Celina’s my daughter. She’s immune to demon sickness.”

Now, Stone was the one who was confused. He looked between the two.

Desir comforted Celina.

Frost looked unbothered.

Stone couldn’t take it. “What do you mean, immune?”

Desir and Frost exchanged a glance, but Frost kept his calm demeanor. “I’m Lucifer’s son. She’s his granddaughter. We are literally Lucifer’s blood. It’s impossible for either of us to be sickened by a demon’s touch.”

Celina's tiny wet hand gripped Desir's shirt. Desir seemed unbothered as he focused on Frost. "I'll take her home."

Another realization hit. It was almost worse than recognizing Desir as a demon. "Wait. Do you not trust me around Celina? You'd literally let a demon leave with her rather than have her near me?" That shattered Stone's heart. Everything had been too much lately. Maybe it might seem like a small thing to anyone else, but knowing Frost didn't want Stone near his daughter was the line, apparently. He hit his breaking point. Stone made a sharp bow with a swollen throat. "It's been an honor to serve." Stone dissipated and reappeared deep in the forest. He couldn't do a job he wasn't trusted to perform. Celeste would have to assign someone else... or not, since apparently, a demon could do his job better than him.

My chest hurts from your pain. What's happened?

I'm fine.

Stone kept his thoughts behind a wall. It was humiliating to know his friends weren't really his friends, and he was seen as a monster. Stone wasn't used to having people look at him the way they did now. He had always been the flirt and jokester. No one had ever taken him seriously, and Stone loved that because he made people smile. Now, this thing had happened. He was the victim, yet everyone saw him as the villain. Whatever the dark one's intentions had been, he definitely accomplished ruining Stone's life.

Stone climbed to the top of the nearest hill. Flowers swayed in the breeze. Stone sat. He stared at the moon. The sound of tiny whispers and moans had a small, sad smile tugging at his lips. Before meeting Lysander, he hadn't heard the fairies all around him. Now, their presence soothed him. He wasn't an outcast in Faerie. He closed his eyes and let the calming sounds wash over him.

The air shifted, and a solid warmth formed at his side. Stone opened his eyes, knowing exactly what he would find.

Lysander took his hand. He didn't speak. Together they gazed at the night sky. The stars were clear here. Sometimes, he missed the old days when city lights didn't pollute the night. The stars had been so clear and bright back then. In Wulfe, there were several similar places where he could find comfort in the night sky. His heart skipped a beat at the thought. He had to screech to a halt and backpedal. There used to be a lot of places in Wulfe where he felt at peace. He wasn't welcome here anymore.

"The sky is even more beautiful in Faerie. Everything is closer to the heavens there. That's why the sheer power of Celeste's creations spawned lives of their own. But our most powerful fairies are born of the stars."

Stone smiled. "Like Stellar." He got it now. Their hierarchy was built on the bright fires in the heavens. "He's in love with you, you know. I felt it the moment I saw his rage at the idea of your leaving him." Stone wasn't jealous. Lysander was his, and he could see Lysander's mind. He would rather pass from this existence than betray Stone.

Lysander leaned his way, relaxing more of his weight against Stone's shoulder. "Stellar and I have been best friends for a long time. I imagine it would hurt him to lose me. After all, it would break me to watch his light die. But our love isn't quite what I think you're picturing. He's my prince. You're my other half."

Stone put his arm around Lysander and tucked him tighter against his side. He kissed Lysander's temple. "Damn right I am." Stone released a long, heavy breath. Some decisions were always harder than others, but this wasn't the first time Stone's life had completely changed course. "Does Stellar have room for one more citizen?"

The sweet smile Lysander gave him proved Stone's thoughts correct. Lysander wanted to continue living in Faerie. The love for his realm shone brightly each time Faerie was mentioned. "I'd rather hoped you'd prefer to live with me over Stellar."

Stone laughed at Lysander deliberately misunderstanding him. "I suppose that sounds good too."

They shared a smile.

Lysander's fell first. "If you'd like to stay here, we can work something out. I understand neither of us saw this coming."

Stone tried to envision staying, but his heart immediately locked down at the idea. Wulfe no longer felt like home. He wasn't needed or wanted here. The way Desir had immediately rushed to take Celina away filled his mind, breaking him all over again. He was done.

"Let's go home."

With one remark, they sat on the same hill with fairy lights surrounding them. Stone looked at the sky. Lysander was right. The stars were nicer here. He took a cleansing breath, letting his past go. The air smelled amazing. He would have a good life here. His gaze moved back to Lysander. How could he not? He had the perfect mate.

Frost sat in silence, rocking Celina while she worked furiously at consuming her bottle. He practically felt Gemini pacing the floor of their new home. It was a mirror image of the cabin before any changes had been made to accommodate patients. They wanted Celina to feel as safe and stable as possible. Plus, they were happy with what they had always had. They didn't want the grand structure Lucifer had tried to create for them. Everything had changed so quickly. Frost just needed a little time alone with his miracle.

His last patient had been seen for the day. When Celina finished her bottle, they would go home. He had set the demons free from their duties for the night. Frost was alone without protection, but he was also more dangerous than the two beasts put together. He didn't need guards right now. Frost had a heavy heart. He couldn't stop picturing Stone's face. Frost had a growing feeling that he was the bad guy. First, Celeste. Now, Stone. He definitely had a way of pushing people away lately. His only excuse was life had been pretty damn overwhelming since moving to Wulfe. Frost genuinely wanted to breathe a little and just savor being a husband and father. Unfortunately, he had a bad feeling that would never happen if he didn't handle all the things he had shoved to the back burner. Frost wasn't a coward. He wouldn't keep acting like one.

"I'd really love to see you, Celeste."

The words had barely died on his lips before she appeared: beautiful and powerful as ever. She looked serene, as if she expected anything. Then, her gaze locked on Celina. She froze to the point of unreadable. Frost supposed that meant his wards had kept her from seeing him—the way he had hoped.

Frost kept rocking. "There's someone you should meet."

Celeste visibly swallowed. "Is it okay—" She motioned between them.

Frost glanced down.

Celina's bottle was empty.

Frost set it aside and stood. "She probably needs to be burped."

Celeste looked as if he handed her a precious jewel as Celina settled in her arms. As he looked on, silent tears spilled over her lashes as she stared down at Frost's miracle baby. "It's been millennia since I've seen my brother speak anything into life that wasn't born of rage and hatred. She's flawless."

Pride and love swelled in Frost's chest. Not only for his daughter, but for the dad and aunt he never expected to have. "We let Lucifer name her. He chose Celina."

A watery chuckle burst from Celeste. "Of course he did. He knows how much I hated when he called me that. It's not a shortened version of anything, but he enjoyed teasing me, pointing out that name is technically one letter shorter than Celeste. I loved it when he smiled at anything at all, so I let him have his fun."

Celeste touched Celina's wrist, and a golden bracelet appeared. "This will grow with you, little one, so you never forget me."

Frost fought the urge to cry. He had never considered how much Celeste had lost when forced to banish her twin. Frost didn't know if she had anyone else.

Maybe her life in heaven had been every bit as lonely as Lucifer's life in Hell.

"The doctor in me wants to point out how dangerous jewelry is on a newborn, but it's you. I'm sure you have way more power than I have education."

Celeste smiled as she moved Celina onto her shoulder to burp her. "You have nothing to worry about. This little girl is an immortal. Like you, she carries the blood of the gods." Celeste focused on him. "That doesn't mean she doesn't need all the love anyone is willing to give her. Even the most powerful beings shrivel without love."

Despite not directly referencing a thing, Frost knew Celeste looked into his heart and saw the weight he carried. Stone had always been good to him. This horrendous thing had happened to him, and everyone—including Frost—failed him now. Frost recalled exactly how Stone looked at Celina. For reasons Frost couldn't see, Stone loved Frost's daughter. He had taken pride in protecting her. That was all he felt from Stone when he was there. Frost had taken a sledgehammer to all of that.

Celeste moved on as if she had meant nothing by her statement. "Thank you for letting me meet her, even if it's only this one time."

Frost blinked, returning completely to the moment. "I don't intend this to be a onetime thing. She's your niece. I want her to have all the family she can handle. All the family I never had." He didn't blame Lucifer or Celeste for not being a part of his life growing up. They hadn't known he existed. But Frost had known a family had been out there somewhere, uncaring of his existence.

More tears spilled down Celeste's face. Her pain was a silent, stoic suffering Frost felt from only standing near her.

Frost couldn't stand it. "I'm sorry I disappeared. It seems I was cursed."

That brought Celeste back to life. "What do you mean? Tell me everything."

The outrage in her tone made Frost smile despite the situation. "It seems Bodhi is back and is—somehow—controlling a dark fae. The fae possessed Stone, using him to get close enough to me to curse me so I doubted my every decision. His spell made me feel overwhelmed by this town and my abilities as a physician. The moment Lucifer took away the enchantment, it was like breathing free air. Every decision I'd made in months was tainted with a doubt I'd never felt in my years as a doctor. I wasn't me."

Celeste nodded along. He could practically see the wheels in her mind turning. "It's likely a dark fae created by the power of his magic. Fae aren't born of the power of nature. They come from the byproducts of Druid magic. Dark produces dark. Light produces light. I can't see Druids. They're unnatural creatures. But there are other beings who can find the dark one. I'll ensure that's handled." She eyed Frost. "It looks as if you're properly warded now. No one can curse or possess you again.

However, I fully intend to keep a closer watch. Nothing and no one will touch my family again."

Frost winced internally. He cleared his throat. "We won't steal too much of your time, then. Gemini and I decided, for Celina's safety, to relocate our home to Hell."

Celeste didn't explode the way he'd expected. She continued to nod along. "Good. Your father is extremely powerful. He can keep you safe. I can't see you there, but I trust my twin. He might no longer want a relationship with me, but that's on me. His hatred could never extend to you or yours. He's too prideful to shun anything he's created."

Frost's smile grew bigger the longer Celeste spoke. She didn't want to claim Lucifer could love him, but just like Frost, she knew he did.

Celina let out a loud belch that sounded like a drunken sailor, making them laugh. Their gazes met. They wore matching grins. One way or another, this family would be a functional one. All it took was one tiny little girl to bridge a gap as old as time. Celina might very well heal them all.

Heaviness sat on Lysander's chest. He felt like he was the only person who recognized how deeply amazing Stone was. His laughing eyes and flirtatious ways were a brightness the human world needed. But they had lost him, and their loss was Lysander's gain. He wished he felt more triumphant. Stone deserved better from the people he cared the most about. Lysander wished he could soothe that hurt. Some things had no balm. That didn't mean Lysander didn't plan to make Stone too happy to think about his friends' betrayal. He fully intended to do that.

He watched Stone trail through the rooms of Lysander's home. Lysander couldn't stand the silence. "We're right next door to Deidra and Jacen. Oh, and Leif and Aspen live almost directly across the street, if you step into the human realm."

Stone flashed him a smile. "That's great." He glanced around. "I've been trying to figure out how to move my things and where they could go. Honestly, you've seen my place. I don't have a ton of shit, since I lived with the King of Scottish vampires back home. When I arrived in Wulfe, I came with verra little. Still, I don't want to clutter your house."

Lysander shook his head and closed the gap between them. He wrapped his arms around Stone. "*Our* house." His gaze swept down Stone's warrior-hardened body. "That accent peeked out for a second a minute ago. Are you feeling homesick? We can visit Scotland anytime you'd like. I can see me flipping up a kilt to find out what's underneath."

Before Lysander had a chance to feel too frisky, someone knocked on the door. They froze and simultaneously turned that way. In unison, they moved to answer. Lysander hadn't been expecting anyone. When he pulled open the heavy wooden door, no one was there, but a stack of things waited. The pile looked large enough to fill a small home.

"What the—"

"That's my stuff," Stone said, cutting him off.

Neither of them moved.

Stone's gaze shot in every direction, openly hunting for the source of the delivery.

"What do you smell?" Lysander didn't know why he whispered. The appearance of Stone's things just seemed too strange on the heels of their earlier discussion—like someone had been watching them.

Stone sniffed the air. "Odd. I smell cotton candy. That's it. No hint of any beings."

"That's..." He had no idea how to finish that sentence.

"Queer," Stone supplied.

Lysander nodded. He couldn't tear his gaze away from the mess. "I suppose we should bring all this inside."

As the words left his lips, boxes lifted and headed straight for them. Stone and Lysander jumped out of the way.

Boxes and furniture flew inside. They danced in the air as they openly hunted for places to put themselves. Neither of them intervened. Even for a fairy, Lysander hadn't seen this brand of magic before. It was as if all Stone's possessions were enchanted.

The whirlwind of items finally stopped. Everything had found a home. They exchanged glances, and Lysander swung the door shut.

"Well, there's one less chore."

A laugh burst from Lysander at Stone's droll statement. "You'll never be able to find anything again."

Stone smiled. It grew brighter by the second. He crowded Lysander's space until he had Lysander trapped against the door. "I bet I can still find the bed." Stone cupped Lysander's cock through his jeans and rubbed. Warmth spread through Lysander's blood. Stone kept tormenting him by unbuttoning Lysander's jeans. "Then again, I don't need a bed, do I? I can blow you right here."

A needy sound came from the back of Lysander's throat. Stone always took Lysander from zero to a hundred in seconds.

His whimper seemed to be exactly what Stone wanted to hear. He dropped to his knees. Lysander's head fell back with a thump against the door. Stone's hot mouth engulfed him. A bright light flared inside his closed eyelids. The heat he produced got warmer. The suction on his dick had Lysander rolling his hips, trying to get deeper and take what he wanted. Stone didn't tease him. He kept a steady pace. Lysander saw the determination inside Stone to make him come as quickly as possible. He wanted to be inside Lysander. The instant he saw that thought, Lysander desperately wanted the same.

"Please. I need you to fuck me."

In a flash, using vampire speed, Stone had him in his arms and braced against the wall. Lysander barely had time to magic up the lube needed before Stone positioned his cock against Lysander's asshole and thrust.

"Tell me if I hurt you."

Oh, he was really about to get fucked. “I dare you to try.”

With permission given, Stone became the vampire he was. He pounded Lysander, easily raising and lowering Lysander on his dick with rapid-pace motions. All Lysander could do was hang on. His first orgasm hit like lightning. He cried his way through, moaning and gasping, before Stone’s fangs struck. The second orgasm made him black out for a second. He hadn’t recovered a single ounce when the third one hit. This time, as he shook with pleasure, Stone joined him over the edge. They fought equally like wildcats to pull every ounce of pulsing pleasure from each other. They kissed and bit, scratched and squeezed. The ecstasy had them on the edge of madness with the way they experienced each other's pleasure combined. Lysander wasn't sure he even breathed any longer. Oxygen was overrated anyhow. Stone's lips swiped his throat where he had just bitten. "I never thought I'd be jealous of the way Weres can mark each other. There's no way for anyone to know you're mine."

The whispered confession caused tears to spring to his eyes. Fairies couldn't scar, and the only time he had seen a vampire have his skin marked was when they were mated to a Were. That in itself was rarer than the most precious of jewels.

"I can mark us in a different way." He kissed Stone's neck. A tattoo appeared beneath his lips. His neck tingled as a similar tattoo etched itself onto him.

Stone stared at Lysander's neck in awe. His gaze moved to hold Lysander's stare. He didn't say anything. Stone looked too stunned to speak. Still holding Lysander, Stone headed for the bathroom. He set Lysander on the edge of the counter, obviously uncaring of the cum Lysander leaked. Stone stared at his neck in the reflection. Lysander's name and lips were deeply branded on his skin in gorgeous fairy ink.

His gaze moved back to Lysander. "I love it." Stone traced his name on Lysander's neck. "Everyone will know you're mine."

Pride swelled in his chest. "I wouldn't have it any other way. You're mine too."

For a moment, they simply held each other's stare. Slowly, matching smiles stretched their lips. Lysander knew Stone felt everything he did. All they needed was each other. They were a beautiful miracle.

Chapter Six

SUNSHINE PEEKED THROUGH THE curtains and highlighted Lysander's skin. He slept peacefully while Stone couldn't stop staring. His skin had a slight glittery hue. He was so fucking beautiful. Being mates was a connection impossible to explain. It was instant love, and no one understood that until they were in Stone's shoes. He had known from the moment they met Lysander was special. Stone had just thought his being a fairy had enchanted him.

Everything in Faerie looked prettier than the human counterpart. It was as if everything was just slightly crisper. Some places were the same except for the surreal sheen. Other places looked like an entirely different world. It hadn't been a hard decision to choose Faerie. The more he thought about it, the righter his choice felt. Lysander was always the most gorgeous creature in any room, but here, goddamn. He left Stone breathless.

As slowly as possible, hoping not to wake Lysander, Stone dragged the covers down, exposing his nude body. He was indescribable, really. When Lysander slept, his entire body relaxed. His wings didn't hide. They looked delicate—as if they'd crumble under the slightest brush. A smirk tugged at

Stone's lips. He had stroked those wings several times. They were strong and so fucking sexy. Plus, stroking them made Lysander moan. That was Stone's favorite pastime.

Chill bumps rose on Lysander's skin.

Stone pulled the covers up again. He wouldn't let Lysander freeze just to satisfy his inner pervert. Damned if he didn't want to kiss him awake and have his way with Lysander's delectable body. Just the thought had him rock hard.

"Mhmm." The sexy sound cut through the air as Lysander stretched like a cat. "I can smell your lust. It's like ambrosia."

Stone smiled at the comparison. Lysander still hadn't opened his eyes. "You're looking verra sexy. You've been teasing me all morning."

Lysander chuckled. "In my sleep? Damn, I'm good." He rolled to his knees and straddled Stone. "Imagine what I can do when I'm awake."

Stone ran his hands up Lysander's thighs. "No need to fantasize. I know exactly what this work of art body can—"

A knock interrupted them.

They froze.

A moment passed. Another knock rang out.

Lysander whispered the obvious. "There's someone at the door."

Curiosity had them donning robes while they exchanged confused glances. Under normal circumstances, Stone would know who graced their stoop only by their scent. He hadn't been inside Faerie long enough to distinguish scents. They answered the door together.

Frost stood on the other side, holding Celina.

Lysander magicked them into being fully dressed.

Stone blinked.

Lysander didn't. "You have a baby in Faerie."

A huge grin lit Frost's face. "To be fair, we live in Hell, so..."

Stone hadn't known that. They stepped back.

Lysander waved frantically. "Get inside before she sees something she shouldn't."

Frost laughed. "She's too young to see something she shouldn't. At her age, she can only see a foot or so away." He stepped inside. Frost had a bulging diaper bag over his shoulder and some sort of small, bouncy chair-bed thing Stone couldn't identify looped over his arm. He passed Celina to Stone—like the exchange was one they made all day. "Here. Hold her. I can't go anywhere anymore without packing the entire house." Frost set everything on the floor. "Not that I'm complaining. I know exactly how lucky I am."

"Speaking of that luck," Lysander said, obviously spotting his opening. "I'm dead curious to know how Gemini and you ended up with a very obviously biologically-yours baby. She looks too much like a mixture of you both to not carry both your genes."

"Best not to ask questions sometimes."

At Frost's response, Lysander and Frost dove into a conversation Stone didn't hear. He couldn't tear his eyes away from Celina. She was beautiful—like staring at a living, breathing true miracle. He was always awed by her. Stone moved to the couch and sat when it didn't seem Frost intended to reclaim Celina. He went back to staring at her.

"Hey, wee one. Did I miss anything good since I saw you last?"

Celina's mouth opened and closed.

Stone smiled. She genuinely looked as if she struggled to tell him a story. Her little fists shot up before moving to her face. She accidentally hit herself trying to get her hand in her mouth. Celina didn't flinch. Instead, she made a small noise. He didn't know it was annoyance or satisfaction. A gold bracelet shimmered on her wrist, catching light in a way that almost looked as if the beams came from within.

Stone touched it. "This is pretty. Already getting gifts from the lads, eh?"

Her ice-blue eyes looked scrunched as she curled her nose. It almost seemed as if she understood him and let her disgust be known.

Stone laughed. "Good for you. Don't put up with any of that nonsense."

Celina made another sound.

It sank in how quiet the room had become. He glanced up. Lysander and Frost were sitting and watching him. They each wore different unreadable expressions.

"Did I miss something?"

Frost smiled. "Not at all. I came to check on my patient. How are you feeling today? Have you had any lingering effects?"

Stone shrugged and went back to looking at Celina. "Nothing I can't handle."

"Nothing you can't handle isn't a no."

At Frost's comment, Lysander jumped in. "He's still not fully back to himself. I can feel the sadness always trying to overwhelm him, but he keeps it hidden."

Since they didn't seem to need him for their conversation, Stone gave his full focus to Celina. "They worry because everyone is scared of me now, but not you, huh."

She smiled.

Joy burst through Stone.

Frost was on his feet. "She's smiling. That's her first smile. Gemini will die when he finds out he missed it. Lucifer..." Frost froze and stared into the distance, as if his mind refused to think of something horrible enough to describe Lucifer missing his grandbaby's first smile.

"Just don't tell them." Lysander sounded pragmatic, as if he didn't understand the big deal. It was a big deal, though, because that first smile had been for him. Stone kind of wanted to cry. He was going through a lot no one could see—not even Lysander. Someone had taken over his life. Worn his face. Used his body and mouth to interact with all his friends. Now no one looked at him the same, and he had done things to make other people hate him. He didn't know what he had done or said or how to fix it, and he was enraged because he couldn't remember any of it. But Celina was all things beautiful and innocent, and she had smiled for him.

Frost practically danced in place. It was more than obvious he wanted to snatch Celina from his arms and get a smile of his own.

Stone didn't want the peace to end, but all things eventually did. He moved his face closer, hoping Celina could see him clearly. "Thank you." He whispered the words. Stone knew everyone would hear, but he wanted Celina to know he spoke only to her.

Celina's little fist shot out. She hit Stone's lips. He didn't take it personally. Stone knew she couldn't control her movements yet. But Stone still stole his chance. He kissed her hand. A jolt shot through him. He felt himself falling as the world around him spun. Memory after memory flowed through him, nearly breaking his mind with the overload. He heard people speaking, but he no longer knew if it was the voices in his head or the people currently with him. His body convulsed, causing him to bite his tongue. Then everything was gone.

Lysander paced. He didn't know what else to do. His brain kept reliving the moment Stone had fallen into a full-blown seizure. He was a vampire—impervious to illnesses. Yet here they were back at Frost's clinic turned mini hospital, and Stone wouldn't wake.

"You look tired. I thought finding a mate brightened our kind."

Lysander spun.

Stellar sat nearby.

Lysander hadn't even heard him arrive. "Where are your guards, Stellar? You can't be running around the mortal realm without protection." He hadn't meant to sound so angry, but he was angry. Life just kept pissing him off, but that wasn't on Stellar. "Sorry. I'm just stressed."

A kind smile lit Stellar's face. "I know. Nonetheless, for your peace of mind, my guards are protecting every possible entry point. There's no need for them to hover." Stellar's expression shifted, showing his concern. "I couldn't let you be alone in your time of need."

Lysander scrubbed his eyes and then looked at the ceiling. He didn't know what to say because he didn't know how he felt. Still, he just spoke with no clue what would pass his lips.

"It's not fair. On stars, I know that sounds childish, but it isn't. Stone is such a good person." Lysander paced as he ranted. "He's so funny and kind. Before this, I was so blinded by his inner light, I didn't even notice him as my mate." He stopped walking a hole into the floor and focused on Stellar. "Oh, and you should see him with Celina.

I don't know what it is, but that little girl loves him so much, and Stone looks at her like the world disappears when she's around."

"I don't know this Celina."

"She's Frost's baby." He went back to pacing. "This bullshit has cost him all his friends and stolen the light from his eyes. And I can't give him children." Lysander said the last bit with every ounce of bitterness in his heart. To have a mate was to love a mate, and Stone had been given a useless partner in life. Having that final truth hit had Lysander freezing and staring into the abyss. He felt helpless.

"What does Frost say about his condition?"

The question tore Lysander from his inner downward spiral. “Nothing. Well, he says Stone is fine. He’s just healing and needs the rest. He’ll wake when he has the energy to do so.”

To his surprise, Stellar chuckled. “That makes him sound like he’s a battery on charge.”

“In a way, he is,” Frost said, strolling into the room. He pulled a penlight from his doctor’s coat and checked Stone’s eyes. Frost listened to his heart and lungs before turning his attention their way. “He’s physically drained from his possession. Stone needs to sleep.” Frost focused on Lysander. Sympathy filled his eyes. “I assure you he’s absolutely fine. Why don’t you two go get some lunch or something? Pacing the floor is only wearing you down. Stone needs you at a hundred percent."

Lysander turned his head. He stared at Stone's sleeping form. Frost was right. Lysander was failing at this too. He couldn't keep this from happening to Stone. Lysander couldn't give him a child, and now he couldn't even let Stone recover properly. His throat swelled.

"You're right. I should go." He should have made the right decision the first time. Lysander shouldn't have let Stone save him, and Lysander shouldn't have claimed him. Stone would be better matched with someone else.

With his heart in his throat, Lysander moved to Stone's side and lightly kissed him. "Goodbye, beautiful." *You deserve a flawless life.*

Lysander straightened and met Stellar's gaze. "What should we do today?"

Stellar didn't move from his seat. His purple gaze stayed locked on Lysander. "We'll stay right here until *your* mate is well, and on his way home with *you.* I did not break my own heart by not fighting for you to watch you be unde-serving."

The words cut to the bone at a time when Lysander felt at his weakest. A tear rolled down his cheek. He wiped it away.

Frost looked between them. "I'll leave you two to hash it out." He moved like he couldn't get away from the drama quickly enough.

An icy chill swept through the room, visibly rocking Frost back on his heels before he made it to the door. Lysander shivered. The walls turned to ice in a slow crawl across every surface. Men shouted in the distance. Stellar shot to his feet, and two glowing swords appeared in his hands from the air he commanded. Frost moved around the room. Sigils appeared on the walls in his wake. Lysander found himself on the bed, hovering over Stone like a mother shielding her child.

"Go to your daughter. Lysander and I are considered warriors of our people. Stone will be safe with us."

Frost didn't budge at Stellar's order. His gaze stayed locked on the doorway. "My daughter is with her dad and grandfather. No one can reach her. This is my clinic. This used to be my home. I dare anyone to try to fuck with me here."

Stellar looked impressed.

Lysander wasn't surprised to learn Frost was a total badass. He was the devil's son, after all. Nothing would get past them.

A sinister laugh rumbled through the room. "You can't fight what you can't see. There's no harming what you can't touch. Stone has something that belongs to me. I'll have it back."

Stellar openly braced to fight. "Nothing of this world is yours. Slink back to your hole. You don't have a single chance against us. The light always swallows the dark."

"Hmm. Some would argue it was the other way around. But I'm not here for philosophical discussions. Stone is my skin. His soul has already been broken. I don't have time to destroy another." A dark mist appeared. It slithered across Lysander's skin, making its way slowly toward Stone. "He has such a delectable body. I'll still let you play with him sometimes."

Lysander couldn't tell if the offer was spoken aloud or was in his head. Either way, Lysander's rage exploded. He tried to grab the shadowy snake, but his fingers slipped through him like smoke.

Another menacing laugh filled the room. "You can't touch me. I'm the sand of doom, filling the bottom half of the ultimate hourglass. I am indomitable."

Without warning, Frost snatched the smoke from where it squeezed Lysander's torso. The creature solidified in his hand, becoming a jet-black serpent.

"Goddamn it, Frost. Every time I'm called here, you're dealing with a snake issue. I don't know how many times is the normal amount, but you must hold some sort of record."

The town's alpha and sheriff, Waylon, stood in the doorway, shaking his head.

Frost laughed. "This is only the third time." He looked thoughtful for a moment. "Fourth time? Either way, not all the calls brought you here." He shrugged. "But I guess Gemini was right about me being the snake whisperer. This does seem to be an inordinate number of times for not working in any snake-driven industry."

The serpent hissed and tried to strike. His every movement was fruitless.

Lysander and Stellar exchanged a look. Everyone seemed unusually unbothered.

Frost turned his attention to the creature he held. "What's your name?"

No response.

A loud sigh burst from Frost. "You couldn't stop talking shit two minutes ago. I can force you to tell me, but there's no reason to get violent."

A royal guardsman came through the door, holding a golden trap. It looked like a normal ten-gallon fish tank, but Lysander saw the magic surrounding it.

"Okay. I guess it's in the tank for you. Things could've been different." He dropped the snake inside. It immediately tried to escape, only to find there was nowhere to go.

"No!" He tried again to no prevail. His beady eyes locked on Frost. "It's Stygian. My name is Stygian. Don't leave me in here. I've already spent a century in a cage."

Frost looked both moved by the plea and unsure. "We've already given you a chance. You should've taken it the last time you left here unharmed. I can't risk this town, and I won't risk my family."

"He'll come with me." The words burst from Stellar like he couldn't hold them another second. He focused on his guard. "Take him home. I'll deal with this."

His guardsman looked as if he fought the need to argue. Lysander wanted to as well, but he knew Stellar. Stellar had his jaw set in a way Lysander had seen hundreds of times. He wouldn't be moved. Stellar was his prince and wouldn't be disobeyed.

The guard gave a slight bow. "Yes, my lord." He vanished along with Stygian.

Stellar focused on Lysander. He was still in full royalty mode. He wasn't Lysander's friend in that moment. Stellar's features softened, as if he heard Lysander's thoughts. "I am always your friend. As such, I'm ordering you to stay glued to your mate. He's suffered enough loss, don't you think?"

Lysander nodded even though he still thought Stone was likely better off without him. The selfish part of him that wanted their mating with every fiber of his being was grateful for the order he couldn't disobey.

Stellar vanished the same as his guard, leaving Lysander still crouched over Stone. Frost and Waylon both looked unruffled.

Frost moved toward the doorway. He turned at the last second and focused on Lysander. "Since you're staying, you should sleep too." He turned off the light.

Lysander wanted to argue. What if the threat wasn't completely neutralized? Stone needed him to stand guard.

Frost chuckled. It was a warm, kind sound that soothed something inside Lysander. "It's almost as if you don't realize you're currently in the safest place in the world. Do you need me to flex some more before I go?"

Lysander's shoulders relaxed. He was being weird. Frost was perfectly capable of defending his clinic. He wasn't even sure why Celeste kept his vamp guards in place. His gaze dropped to Stone's beautiful face. Not that he was complaining. Being Frost's security had brought Stone to him.

"Sleep," Frost repeated. This time, an odd echo vibrated behind his command.

It hit Lysander. Stone hadn't awoken once during the drama. Not even when Lysander pounced on him. Now he knew why. As he crumpled on top of Stone's body, Lysander saw it all. Frost controlled everything.

The halls of his family's home echoed with emptiness. Considering dozens of people lived there, and the place was filled with excess, Stellar knew the sound always came from his heart. He had lived a damn long life. Things rarely changed, and even more rarely for the better. He was bored with existence. Stellar grew more bitter by the day. He hadn't realized exactly how bad things had gotten until he watched Lysander fall in love with someone else. The entire experience had been like seeing the final petal of the most beautiful rose wither away.

Once inside his bedroom, Stellar still didn't draw a single breath of relief. Taurus stood guard inside. Stellar felt the man's sparkling yellow eyes following his every move. His disapproval practically clogged the air.

"I don't want to hear it."

Taurus didn't respond. That was worse than a lecture.

Stellar peeled off his shirt and tossed it aside. "You think I'm an idiot for bringing him here. Maybe I am. But he's bound and I'm no weakling."

"I've said nothing. Those were your words."

Stellar popped the button on his soft leather pants. His temper frayed, but he held his tongue. It wasn't Taurus' fault he was in a bad headspace tonight.

Warm lips touched his shoulder.

Stellar automatically grabbed the edge of the dresser in front of him as his knees weakened. His eyes closed, and a shaky breath escaped him. Taurus was a warrior born of fire. Even from behind closed lids, Stellar could picture Taurus. From the orange hair, which he kept in a messy bun, to his flashing yellow eyes. Stellar could probably list his every measurement and paint his body in the dark. He craved the meal Taurus offered.

"As much as I love a good show, I much prefer to join."

The caustic words had Stellar spinning toward the voice. From the magic cell in the corner, a solid shadow leaned against the bars. His body was a perfect outline with no features. He might have been terrified by the sight if he hadn't dealt with Stygian's type before.

Stellar snorted. "As fun as I'm sure that would be, I'll have to deny your request. Sex isn't quite as enjoyable when you're worried about having your throat sliced the entire time."

A wicked chuckle rumbled from the cage. "I disagree. Nothing like adrenaline to keep things exciting."

Stellar shook his head. "Still, I prefer a partner with a body."

He tossed a glance Taurus' way, expecting commiseration.

Taurus stared back at him with a closed expression.

Stellar sighed. "It seems I'm disappointing everyone tonight. Sleep it is, I suppose."

"I love your confidence, thinking I'll let you rest."

Stellar felt an evil smile tugging at the corners of his mouth, stretching his lips. A spark of life lit inside him at the challenge Stygian presented. "Your confidence is astounding. I love the way you think I can't make you do anything and everything I want."

"Actually, I'm banking on that."

Stellar couldn't stop smiling. He loved a good banter session. People rarely tried to test him.

"My lord."

Stellar didn't look Taurus' way. He didn't need a lecture. "You can go."

He felt the heat of Taurus' silent anger as he headed for the door. Stellar would make it up to him. Taurus wasn't just a guard to him. He was Stellar's friend.

Tonight, Stellar didn't think a friend was what he needed. Judging by the power and excitement coursing through his veins, Stellar had a feeling he had found what he sought: an enemy.

Chapter Seven

MOONBEAMS SHONE BRIGHTLY THROUGH the trees, giving the forest an almost strobe light effect as he ran through the woods, using his vampire speed. Stone had no idea what he fled. He only knew he couldn't stop moving. The scent of blood and tiny hearts beating assailed his senses. He was hungry in a way he hadn't been since he was a fledgling. If he stopped moving, he would do something terrible. Stone didn't want to harm anyone else.

Sunshine suddenly parted the trees. The moon was all but forgotten. His pace slowed. Stone didn't have the same energy in the daylight. In the light, nothing looked the same. His anxiety vanished. The only blood he smelled was the sweetest of drinks. The only heartbeat beat for him. Standing ankle-deep in a creek, Lysander kicked through the water. His glow outshone the sun. The smile he wore was all Stone saw.

"I knew you'd come." Stone had no idea why he said that. But as the words had left his lips, Stone realized exactly how true they were.

Eyes, a mixture of blue and green, turned his way. Lysander's smile didn't dim. "Hey, gorgeous. I'll always come for you."

Stone smiled at the innuendo. "Well, I mean, you should. I work hard to make you happy."

Lysander's eyes sparkled with happiness. He bit his bottom lip as his gaze swept down Stone's body. "Hard indeed."

Yeah, there was likely no hiding his erection. Lysander didn't even have to touch him to bring him to life.

Lysander's expression changed. His bottom lip shot out. "Too bad this is only a dream. You won't feel my touch for real here."

Stone looked around. He supposed he had known that. Everything had a dream-like quality. Nothing looked solid or real, except Lysander. He saw every inch of him.

"We should definitely wake up so I can show my appreciation for having you as my better half."

"Sorry, can't."

Lysander made the claim nonchalantly, as if Stone should have noticed by now that he couldn't wake. He fought harder to get back to the real Lysander.

"I am the real Lysander. We're connected with each other's minds, remember, and Frost knocked me out too."

Stone moved closer to the water's edge. "Too? What do you mean? Why would he do that?"

Lysander climbed onto a large rock and jumped toward Stone.

Stone automatically caught him. Suddenly, Stone didn't care so much about the whys. Lysander felt very real in his arms. "On second thought, what's the rush? As long as we're together, right?"

Lysander brightened. "Exactly." His smile slipped away. He wrapped his arms around Stone's neck, as if scared he would get away. "What do you remember?"

Stone sifted through his memories, trying to recall the last thing he had done. His chest warmed. "I was spending time with Celina."

Lysander nodded. "And then?"

Stone shook his head. "Then nothing. I kissed her wee hand and—" Stone froze. He didn't need to relive the moment, but he knew he would sound mad. "I think she healed me."

Lysander looked taken aback. "You went into a seizure. I'm not sure that can be considered healing."

"I don't know anything about that, but I suddenly recalled everything: who possessed me and what Stygian had done while wearing my skin." Sadness swept through him. "It's not good."

Lysander didn't hesitate. "It wasn't you, and you don't need to worry about any of that. Stellar contained him and is taking care of that. You're free, and no one blames you for the things he did. It wasn't you."

Stone found himself smiling again. "I know. Celina told me."

To his surprise, Lysander didn't look happy about his confession. His gaze slid away. Stone got a blast of unhappiness that nearly took him to his knees. It wasn't his.

Stone didn't want any more dark times. Unfortunately, he obviously failed his mate. "Talk to me. I need my life back, Lysander. Please don't make me worry if I'm doing something wrong. I can't take anything else."

Lysander shifted uncomfortably. He didn't meet Stone's stare. "I can feel how much you love Celina."

A nervous chuckle escaped Stone. “Surely you don’t think you have to compete with a baby. That’s—”

“No,” Lysander said in a rush, as if horrified by even the suggestion. “I can’t give you that. You won’t have that life with me.”

Stone was confused as fuck. “Have what life?” He didn’t think he was dense or anything. Lysander had him blocked, and he possessed the magic to hold Stone at bay. He spoke in circles, and Stone didn’t know how to play this game. He had never loved anyone with the burning intensity he felt for Lysander. There was no one else out there for him. If Lysander didn’t want a life with him, there would never be anyone again.

"Do you mean that?"

Stone blinked. Lysander made him feel dumb as hell. "Mean what?"

Lysander didn't back down. "All the thoughts you're having about loving me and there being no one else? I can't see you giving up a carnal life, not even for me."

He actually had Stone a little angry. It felt like Lysander doubted him in several ways and kept those feelings to himself. "I love you. That's bigger than everything. You're my partner for eternity. I don't need anything else."

"Not even a child of your own?"

The bark of laughter that burst from Stone almost came from his core, but he still apologized when Lysander's closed expression didn't change. It was obvious he felt the need to protect himself against this matter.

Stone forced himself to take the topic seriously for Lysander's sake. "I'm sorry. You just caught me off guard. I'm not father material. I'm way too needy and selfish. A child deserves better than me refusing to spend my time with anyone other than you."

"But I've seen you with Celina. There's a parent inside you."

Stone had to focus on not rolling his eyes. "There absolutely is not. Now, a rich uncle who spoils kids and sends them right back home. I might be that guy, and that's a big might. Celina is special, and I can't explain that. But she's also exactly where she needs to be: with the family who made her that way. Not once in my life have I looked at another child and wanted any part of them. That probably makes me sound like a bastard, but—"

"You're too much of a free spirit," Lysander finished for him. His smile had reappeared.

"I planned to say whore, but tomato, tomato."

Before Stone saw it coming, Lysander grabbed his junk and massaged him through his jeans. It wasn't exactly a gentle caress. "Those days are gone. You belong to me. This is real love. Don't fuck it up." Lysander's hard expression and possessiveness was hot as hell.

Lust ricocheted through him. He hauled Lysander against him by his perfect globes. Stone squeezed, massaging Lysander's ass while using the momentum to rock against him. "That's a two-way street. I see the way everyone looks at you and how you use that to your advantage. Utilize what you've got, but you best recall you're mine and no one will ever love you the way I do."

"Not even an issue." Lysander shot forward and covered Stone's mouth with his. Nothing could have thrown ice water on the situation faster. The move reminded him that this was still just a dream. As the scenery surrounding them faded, he wondered if any of it had been real.

The moment Lysander's eyes shot open, he rolled, covering Stone's body, and magicked them home before Frost could appear and knock them out again. He knew Stone still needed to stay in bed, but Lysander could keep him there. At home. In their bed. They were past due for a honeymoon stage, where they shut out the world. He wouldn't tolerate any interruptions. Celina had not only healed Stone, but she had made sure he understood he still had his friends.

Lysander would try to wrap his head around the Celina stuff at a later time. Literally nothing else mattered right now.

The moment Stone's back hit the bed with Lysander's body covering him, his eyes shot open. For a second, he looked like a trapped animal before he focused on Lysander. His muscles relaxed beneath Lysander's hands. Stone's features softened. "Hey, baby."

Dear King, Lysander loved him. "Hey. Did you have a nice nap?"

A wicked smile stretched Stone's lips. "I had a dream I didn't want to end, but this is better."

Lysander waggled his eyebrows. "Ah, it was that kind of dream."

"You should know. You were there."

Lysander laughed. He couldn't help it. There had never been this much happiness in his life. It had nowhere to go. "Maybe."

"I knew it!" Stone shouted the words, making Lysander's ears ring with his enthusiasm. "How do you keep doing that? Connected in mind or not, I don't think I could pull that off." He looked thoughtful for a moment. "At least I don't think I can."

Lysander lifted one shoulder in a half shrug. "If you put your mind to it, I'm sure you could. But I'm a fairy. We can move freely through all realms. Everyone wants us." He added the last bit using his most sexual tone.

Stone flipped.

Lysander found himself beneath a very hungry-looking vampire. "But only one being matters now." Stone shoved his hand beneath Lysander's ass and squeezed. He lowered his head and swiped his lips against Lysander's mouth in a featherlight kiss. Then Stone rolled out of the bed as if nothing had happened. "I can feel your hunger. What would you like to eat? I'll make you something."

A growl rose in Lysander's throat. Stone drove him crazy, and he knew it. With barely any effort, Lysander lunged. He hauled Stone back into bed and straddled him. "You're right. I'm starving—for you." He easily tore away Stone's clothes with no shame. Life would bend to him. No more interferences. "Give me that dick."

The way Stone laughed at the demand might have driven him off into a pout any other time. But Stone was right. Lysander needed to feed. He needed real food too, but carnal energy was his top priority. Still, he couldn't let Stone get the upper hand. "I thought you worried about my well-being. Maybe I'll just—" Lysander made a move, as if he meant to leave the bed.

A scary sound burst from Stone as he attacked. The wisps of the clothes they had left fell away in shreds with the slightest tugs from Stone. Just like last time, Lysander barely had time to use his magic to prepare before Stone was inside him. "I'm the only one who has what you need." Stone ripped into Lysander's throat and drank. The orgasm of all orgasms lit the room. No doubt he had probably blinded Stone with the way he glowed, but Stone didn't stop making love to him, and that was what it was. His explosion had blocked out everything except the way his body felt. Now he recognized how Stone had gone from violence to tenderly rocking inside him while Lysander had been trying to hang on to his sanity.

Lysander's chest burned with emotion. They felt connected. He wanted to say everything in his heart.

Tell me.

The soft demand brushed his mind like a butterfly kiss. Lysander didn't play dumb. He knew what Stone sought. "I love you."

The way Stone melted inside at Lysander's words completely rocked Lysander. He saw and felt how deeply Stone needed to hear Lysander's emotions spoken aloud. He ached for what only Lysander could give him.

"I love you too."

It seemed Stone wasn't the only one who needed those words. When the soft declaration caressed his brain, another blazing quake had him whimpering and chanting Stone's name. This time, Stone was right there with him, but Lysander needed Stone to fly higher than ever. He bit Stone's shoulder. The waves that crashed through Stone nearly took out Lysander's sanity. Maybe they were brand new at this mate thing, but Lysander thought they were beautiful.

The sweetest kiss swiped his skin. "Me too, baby. Me too."

Lysander drew a steadying breath through his nose. He kind of loved having Stone in his head, listening to his thoughts. That wasn't something he had considered. But Lysander felt less alone in the world. Until Stone filled a hole in his life, Lysander hadn't noticed how much had been missing.

"What should we do next?"

A loud laugh burst from Lysander at Stone's question. He was deliriously happy. "We should probably get some real food in us. Don't you think?"

With Stone draped over his body, he felt the way Stone shook when he laughed. "Are you telling me a fairy and a vampire can't live on sex alone?"

"Well, I can," Lysander taunted.

Stone snorted.

Lysander couldn't stop smiling. "As much as I know you could survive on just my blood, you need your strength. I intend to be a harsh taskmaster, expecting to be serviced often."

Stone rolled to his side, chuckling. "Damn. I'm glad I found you."

Lysander held his stare. "Me too."

They shared a smile.

Lysander already knew they would climb from this bed, and he would cook for Stone. Afterward, Stone would try to seduce him while Lysander played hard to get before giving in. It would be a short fight. When he thought about the future, that was all he saw. Days, years, and centuries of love. Nothing had ever sounded better.

Chapter Eight

STONE HATED HE WAS nervous, but he was. Before his possession, Stone had always just sort of shown up to work each day. It wasn't like he'd had anything else to do, really. He didn't actually need sleep unless he was injured. A lot of his kind slept just to have a way to fill hours in the day. Forever was a long time to entertain yourself. Being newly mated, Stone didn't need to find ways to do something other than work or sleep. Lysander kept him busy now. A smile stretched his lips just thinking about all the ways Lysander could entertain him.

Unfortunately, Stone couldn't stay on his honeymoon forever. It wasn't fair to expect anyone else to step in so he could stay home—not that he believed Frost needed him at all. Still, Celeste had asked this of him when Frost had come into his powers. He supposed he would stick to the duty until she said otherwise. He felt honor-bound, and—truthfully—it was his honor to serve. Most especially, he wanted to see Celina.

While Lysander had assured him Stone had somehow managed to pass Celina to Frost before ending up on the floor, Stone still wanted to check on her. He hated the thought of him going into a seizure while holding her. Plus, Stone wanted to see her smile again. Stone picked up his step at just the thought.

As he broke through the woods into the clearing behind Frost's house, Fen stepped in his path, stopping him from going any farther. "Damn, man. I've been waiting for an age for you to come back. What's kept you away?"

Despite his concerns about any lingering hard feelings, Stone smiled. Fen had been his friend for a long time. They had come to America together from Scotland. He had hoped if anyone wanted to stay friends, it would be Fen. "My mate."

A smile exploded across Fen's face. "I can't even imagine how hard it is to keep up with a fairy. Maybe not for you, though. With your reputation, I'm sure you're nae disappointed."

The giant red-haired warrior had once been the personal guard of the vampire king of Scotland. If anyone had the temperament to hold a grudge, it was Fen. Yet he didn't seem to harbor any ill will. "I have to admit he's the perfect match for me."

Fen tilted his head to one side and eyed the glittery tattoo on Stone's neck. "That's a heck of a mating mark. Unique. We find our ways, I suppose."

Stone had no idea what that meant, but he had some shit to say before Fen got away. "I'm sorry for everything I said while possessed. Truly. I hope you know I'm thrilled you found your other half, and I hate that bastard used my body to try to make you doubt the strength of your union. Kyrie seems very sweet. He's exactly who I would've pictured you ending up with."

Fen shook his head. His expression turned serious in a way Stone hadn't seen in decades. "If anyone understands what you've been through, it's me. I literally got caught in a skirmish between the gods. They almost ruined my entire life. I know you had no control." He grabbed Stone's shoulder and squeezed. "I've also known you for a long time, so I'm verra sorry I didn't suspect anything. You would never hurt anyone." Fen shifted from foot to foot. "In fact, that's why I hoped to see you. You're the one owed an apology. If I hadn't gotten so caught up in my own drama, I could've helped you. I should have helped you."

Stone's throat swelled. He hadn't known what he needed to hear to lessen his guilt, but Fen had said it. Fen could never know what his apology meant to him. "I appreciate it." He hoped things went as smoothly when he apologized to Leif and Aspen. They were another couple he had used to stir discontent. Guards distracted by their drama were less likely to notice anything wrong with Frost.

Fen hugged him. The embrace meant the world. They were warriors. Soldiers for the Goddess of Creation. They didn't hug, but they had lived long enough to know all that masculinity bullshit was just that: bullshit. While Celina made him realize nothing had been his fault, it was still nice to have this off his chest.

The thought of Celina had him taking a step back. "I guess I'd better get inside."

Fen fell into step next to him as he headed toward the cabin. "Have fun with all that. Weird things are afoot with all these demons around. I assume Celeste isn't worried about them, but the hair stays standing on my neck."

Stone nodded along. He got it. "Are we protecting Frost or is he protecting us? I'm not sure any longer."

Fen's hands lifted and fell. "I traveled many times to see the king of the Americas when I guarded King Lachlan. As powerful as King Jonathan is, even he has security. No one is infallible."

That was true.

At the back door, Fen moved to stand next to it, taking up his post for the day. Fen gave him a nod and headed inside.

Before the cabin's overnight transformation into a miniature hospital for the supernatural, the back door was how people arrived from the mirror land. Now it looked as if that entrance had been given its own waiting room.

Stone eyed everything he passed. This time when he saw Moroder, the demon didn't even acknowledge him. On his way down the hall, where he heard Frost's voice, he passed Desir's office. With his feet on his desk, his ankles were crossed. He looked relaxed and at home. His light blue gaze followed Stone's every move as he passed. Without a word exchanged, he felt the lust pouring from Frost's new office manager. Stone shook his head. He wondered how anything got done with actual lust hanging out in the building.

Finally, Stone came to Frost's office. Frost sat behind his desk, tapping away on a laptop. Gemini sat in the corner, rocking Celina. Her cheek was squished against Gemini's chest, and her tiny fingers gripped tightly around a lock of Gemini's long hair. With her mouth slightly open, she slept peacefully.

"Oh no." Stone said the words quietly as he strolled into the room. "I'm too late. She's already milk drunk and sleeping it off."

Frost smiled.

Gemini chuckled. "Don't worry. Give her a few. She'll be screaming for more."

Stone pulled a chair close and sat. "She's growing like a weed. I swear she gets bigger every time I see her."

"I should hope so. She keeps all of Hell awake all night, demanding bottles."

At Frost's statement, Stone looked closer at Gemini and him. They had dark circles under their eyes. It looked as they hadn't slept in weeks. He wondered if they ever got a break. As if proving his suspicions correct, all hell broke loose.

Fen came skidding into the doorway, looking panicked. "A very pregnant Were just came through the door." His announcement sent everyone scrambling. The howls of pain that rent the air were terrifying.

Gemini focused on him with a panicked look. He passed Celina Stone's way. "I need you to take Celina. If this ends badly, there's always a risk the pack will turn on Frost. Just lock yourself in here. Frost will ward the door."

Frost was already gone, rushing to aid his patient.

Stone didn't ask questions. He just did as told. While he didn't think any of the Weres in Wulfe would harm a baby, grief and pain could be an ugly thing. Since it was common for Weres and their babies not to survive childbirth, Gemini was smart in not risking anything.

The moment he was alone with no instructions, his gaze dropped to the child he held. He knew virtually nothing about taking care of a baby. "Well, fook."

"*Tsk. Tsk.* Language."

Icy fingers of fear ran down Stone's spine at the sudden appearance behind him. He spun. In the back of his mind, Stone recognized Lucifer was Celina's grandfather, and—supposedly—he had freed Stone from Stygian. But thoughts and reality were two very different ballgames. He had never stood toe to toe with the king of Hell. Stone never expected to do so, yet here he was. Lucifer hovered over him. He was tall as fuck. Stone realized Celina had some of his features as well.

Lucifer stroked Celina's cheek. "That's because my son looks like me."

That one caught Stone off guard. Not only because Lucifer obviously read his mind, but Stone hadn't considered that. To be fair, his brain didn't want to work.

Lucifer's gaze lifted from Celina and met his stare.

Everything inside Stone wanted to run. Only his pride saved him. Of course, it might have been terror keeping his feet glued to the ground.

"She loves you. You don't talk to her like she's a baby."

Stone blinked. He didn't know how to respond. That seemed such an odd statement to make. Lucifer had said that like Celina had told him about Stone.

Lucifer turned away and grabbed a baby bag from the floor. He set it on Frost's desk and dug through it. "Come here. I have souls to torture. You need to know how to take proper care of my grandbaby. Labor is a long process, especially for a Were."

Everything about that assertion was absolutely terrifying. This was the devil's granddaughter. He had to make sure no harm came to her, or it would be the last thing he did. Not that he would let anything happen to Celina. He would die first.

Blue eyes, eyes of the gods, focused on him. "That's one of the many reasons I'm trusting you with this. I see your heart. You'd give your life to keep her safe. Plus, you're one of my twin's warriors and all that nonsense. Yada yada. Whatever." He pulled an empty bottle from the bag and a bottle of formula. "This is premixed, so it's fairly idiot-proof. She's up to six ounces." He pointed out the lines, showing the six. "See. Idiot proof."

He motioned for Stone to hand Celina to him. He had never been more torn. It was the devil. It was her grandfather. He was her devil grandfather. Stone fought a hysterical laugh. Maybe his mind had snapped. He passed Celina to Lucifer. Stone watched as Lucifer stole several kisses before pulling a padded thing from the bag.

"I'm about to ruin her day, but you need a crash course." He set Celina on the pad and went to work on changing her diaper. Stone studied every move. This was important to him. He wanted to take good care of Celina. Stone ignored the way Celina screamed and fought. He blocked out who taught him what he needed to know. Nothing mattered but ensuring Celina got proper care.

Lucifer snapped her pajamas back together and passed her to Stone. "She'll settle down as soon as she's warm again."

If Stone stayed focused on Celina, he somewhat forgot he was alone with the king of Hell. "Say you've got this."

At Lucifer's demand, Stone snapped to attention. "I've got this." The way Celina still cried belied his words. He didn't know how to stop her from making that sound.

Lucifer held his stare for a minute. It wasn't comfortable. "Feed her. She's hungry."

"On it."

Lucifer gave him a sharp nod and stole another kiss from Celina. “Papaw will be back later.”

Celina settled down. Her cries turned into fussiness.

The moment Stone worked one-handed to make her a bottle, she calmed.

“Oh, I see how it’s going to be. As long as you’re in charge, then no one gets hurt.”

Celina smiled.

Stone melted. This one little girl really had everyone she met wrapped around her finger. Stone wasn’t the least bit mad about it.

If Lysander hadn't heard Stone in his head for the past sixteen hours, he would have gone after him sooner. Another successful Were baby slept in a new momma's arms. It was a good day. As always, when Lysander popped onto Frost's property, alarms sounded. They were immediately silenced by Leif. Leif nodded his way, but not a single vampire moved from their post. Everyone looked on edge—like they were extra on guard tonight.

With a mental shrug, Lysander strolled inside. There were no demons on duty. The place was eerily silent. Stone had asked Lysander to come to him. While Stone's thoughts had been strangely blank on the matter, Lysander hadn't been suspicious in any way. He hoped the request was a case of Stone missing him. Now that he was here, something felt slightly off. There was an odd static in the air that crackled. It wasn't magic. It was pure, unadulterated power. Lysander picked up the pace.

By the time Frost's office came into view, Lysander felt like he had waded his way through the power hanging in the air. Fairies were extremely strong, but they were also light. They felt any change in the environment. A golden glow hit Lysander first. It wasn't like he needed to shield his eyes, but it was noticeable. Then Lysander saw him. A golden god with molten swirling eyes. Black wings draped the floor. Some of the world's most notorious vampires stood guard over him. They seemed twice the size of normal vamps. Unsure of what to do, Lysander gave a small wave.

Frost, Gemini, and Stone sat nearby, looking completely at ease with the huge, winged creature. Audor leaned against the wall right inside the doorway, openly on guard.

"Hi."

Lysander blinked when the man spoke. He sounded... normal.

The glowing stranger laughed. "That's oddly nice. No one has thought of me as normal in a long time. We've been waiting for you."

He could read minds. Lysander wasn't surprised. Everything about him screamed godly power. Lysander eased Stone's way.

Before he made it, Stone stood. He snagged Lysander by the waist and reclaimed his chair with Lysander on his lap. Stone kissed him. It was a sweet brushing of lips on lips. "Hey, baby."

Lysander nearly melted at the sugary greeting.

Stone gestured toward the winged beast. "This is King Jonathan."

Jonathan gave him a nod of greeting and waved toward the men flanking him. "My mates. Cin and Niall." He motioned toward two giant Scots and a demon lining the wall. "Faol, Lire, and Dougal." Each man nodded at him as they were introduced. "I'm here with a new-assignment order for Stone. As his mate, you have the right to be here for any commands he receives."

Lysander hadn't known that, but he appreciated the inclusion. He looked at Stone to check his reaction since his mind was blank. Stone loved Wulfe. If asked to serve elsewhere, he didn't know how Stone would feel. Lysander wouldn't exactly love it either. Their home might be in Faerie, but it was *here* in Faerie.

Jonathan didn't leave them hanging for long. He focused on Stone. "Audor has already agreed to step into your role as Frost's personal guard."

Ouch. They already had a plan to replace him.

"Celeste recognizes your loyalty and hates to ask more of you, but she'd like—if you're willing—for you to become Celina's personal guard when she's in this realm."

Lysander's gaze shot to Stone and then to Frost and Gemini. Frost and Gemini looked unruffled. He hoped they had been consulted. If not, they were obviously fine with the decision.

"It is my honor to serve." Stone sounded so professional—like the lifelong soldier he was.

Everyone looked at him. Lysander had no clue why. He hadn't been ordered to do shit, nor did he answer to Celeste. "What?"

A huge smile exploded across Jonathan's face at his open confusion. His pot-of-gold swirling eyes crinkled in the corners. "Do you give your permission?"

"Oh." He felt out of his depth. "If this is what Stone wants, I'm fine with it. He loves Celina and would protect her with his life." As Lysander said the words, it dawned on him why he was consulted. Guarding Celina would be a lifelong high-risk position. There might come a day when Stone literally died protecting Celina. He imagined the great-niece of a goddess and granddaughter of a god would be a prize for anyone looking to strike against the heavens. Even after recognizing why he was being asked to agree, Lysander felt no different. Stone loved that little girl. There would be no more ferocious guard than Stone. He would support Stone in this.

Jonathan's smile never dimmed. "I see you, too, are a powerful warrior. Do you know I've never met a fairy?"

He seemed very nice. His observation made Lysander smile. "Crazy. I've never met whatever you are before either."

Jonathan and his entourage all laughed. He swiped his eyes as if he found Lysander hilarious. "I'm a Nephilim."

Well, shit. Lysander hadn't been wrong about the power thing. Nephilim were born of an angel and human. They were more powerful than most anything in heaven or on earth. An amazing pick to be king, especially if he was as kind as he seemed.

"It's very nice to meet you. Maybe I can give you and your mates a glimpse into Faerie one of these days." They looked to be a virile group. He imagined they would enjoy themselves in Lysander's realm.

"I'd love that." He stood. "For now, I have to get home. My brother is currently decorating a surprise party that I'm not supposed to know about for my birthday."

Everyone groaned, including Frost and Gemini.

Jonathan laughed. "Don't worry. I intend to pretend I didn't know. You know Tam is horrible at secret keeping."

Frost stood. "We'll get Celina and meet you there."

The group dispersed, chatting the entire way.

Lysander waited until they were completely alone to turn sideways on Stone's lap. "Everyone's gone. You can stop hiding your thoughts now."

Stone looked baffled. "I'm not." His features cleared. He chuckled. "Celeste's request wiped my brain clean. I guess I still haven't completely recovered from the shock. I know you don't realize it, but this assignment is the highest of honors. Celeste could've chosen anyone to be her niece's sentry. This is a massive..." Stone didn't seem to know how to finish that thought—like there wasn't a strong enough description.

"Compliment to your character," Lysander supplied. "I don't know why you're surprised. No one outside of her family could possibly care for her the way you do. As much as I pray we never find out, I know you wouldn't hesitate to give your last breath to save her from any threat. You're the right choice."

A sweet and slightly embarrassed-looking smile touched Stone's lips. "I'm humbled."

"I am too." Confusion crossed Stone's features. Lysander didn't make him ask or dig through Lysander's mind. "Being blessed with you as my mate makes me wonder why. You're obviously considered one of Celeste's most trusted guards. Why would she choose me for you? I've done nothing to deserve this."

Stone's sexy gaze moved over Lysander's face. "I can't believe Celeste expects anyone to earn love. You're my other half. I'm not special. If anyone has no idea why they're so blessed, it's me. You could've had royalty as a mate. But we were given each other, and I'm so damn grateful for that every second of the day." Stone always made Lysander feel warm all over, inside and out. It had always been that way from the first moment they met.

"We should go home, don't you think?"

A wicked smile stretched across Stone's lips. "Definitely."

"None of that," Gemini said, strolling into the room carrying all of Celina's stuff. "You two are going with us. Guardian and all that. Wherever Celina goes in this realm, you do too."

Lysander might have been annoyed if he weren't curious as hell about the king and, apparently, there was a brother too. Plus, he always enjoyed a good party. Stone and he exchanged a longing look, but they were also equally excited by the opportunity. They smiled. Lysander scrambled from Stone's lap. Everything about life felt brand new since their pairing. They would savor this blessing together.

About the Author

CHARITY PARKERSON IS AN award-winning and multi-published author with several companies. Born with no filter from her brain to her mouth, she decided to take this odd quirk and insert it in her characters. One of her greatest loves is writing morally gray characters. You'll find them scattered throughout her hundreds of titles.

*Nine-time Readers' Favorite Award Winner

*2015 Passionate Plume Award Finalist

*2013 Reviewers' Choice Award Winner

*2012 ARRA Finalist for Favorite Paranormal Romance

*Five-time winner of The Mistress of the Darkpath

Connect with her online:

*Sign up for her newsletter: https://bit.ly/charityparkersonnewsletter

*Join her readers' group on Facebook: http://bit.ly/CharitysTribe

*Website: https://www.charityparkerson.com

*A list of her social media accounts and giveaways all in one place: http://hy.page/charityparkerson

www.ingramcontent.com/pod-product-compliance
Lightning Source LLC
LaVergne TN
LVHW010652110826
845149LV00014B/3044

* 9 7 8 1 9 5 9 5 7 6 9 2 1 *